AN ALTERNATE 1945—AND ADOLF HITLER HAS THE BOMB . . .

"Hold it right there," Queghan said. "You want me to sit in the RECONPAN lab conversing with the brain of Adolf Hitler?"

"Not only conversing. You must try to project yourself into this mythical other world. We don't know what's going to happen there and neither do we know how this alternative scenario will work out in the end." Karve looked at him intently.

"But RECONPAN can provide that information."

"That's true. What it can't do is influence events in any way. We are, to use your phrase, in the position of an unfortunate bystander—unless somenow we can intervene and shape those events."

"So you want me to project myself into this other world?"

Karve raised his head and smiled, rather bleakly. "I'm asking you to become the anti-matter man," he said.

THROUGH THE EYE OF TIME

The "Q" Series by Trevor Hoyle, available from Ace Science Fiction:

#1. Seeking the Mythical Future (March 1982)

#2. Through the Eye of Time (April 1982)

#3. The Gods Look Down (May 1982)

THE SECOND BOOK OF THE "Q" SERIES

THROUGH THE EYE OF TIME

TREVOR HOYLE

SF
ace books
A Division of Charter Communications Inc.
A GROSSET & DUNLAP COMPANY
51 Madison Avenue
New York, New York 10010

THROUGH THE EYE OF TIME

An ACE Book

First North American Edition

First Ace printing: April 1982

Published Simultaneously in Canada

2 4 6 8 0 9 7 5 3 1
Manufactured in the United States of America

Acknowledgements

The following have proved invaluable as reference sources and also as inspiration for a number of the "concepts" which appear in this book: *The Last Days of Hitler* by H.R. Trevor-Roper (Macmillan, 1947; Pan, 1968); *The Double Cross System* by J. C. Masterman (Yale University Press, 1972, Sphere, 1973); *Einstein* by Banesh Hoffmann (Hart-Davis, MacGibbon, 1973; Paladin, 1975); and not least C. G. Jung's *Structure and Dynamics of the Psyche*.

I should also like to thank Pam Yeowart for her help with the German translations.

For Nick Webb—a human, not to say humane, editor.

Contents

"I am now convinced that theoretical physics is actual philosophy."

Max Born

"Nach links und ein bisschen nach unten. Ach, das ist besser!"*

Adolf Hitler

(*"To the left and down a bit. Ah, that's better!")

In the beginning the heavens were void.

Matter did not exist, and without matter neither time nor space. Nothing stirred in the entirety of non-Creation and minus time.

Questions too, like the heavens, were void. There was no one to ask them and no one to answer, so the questions remained unasked and unanswered.

Then into this cosmic enigma a question did appear: a question-mark composed of a single point of light: the Primeval Atom. With light came energy, and with energy matter, and with matter space, and with space time.

The Holy Trinity:

Time.

Matter.

Space.

The universe had been born.

Soon after its birth—one one hundred thousand billion billionth of a second—the point of light was at a temperature of one thousand billion billion degrees. The point of light began to cool.

At one ten thousandth of a second after Creation, at a temperature of one thousand billion degrees, the first species of particle came into existence:

The Hadron.

Still later in the evolutionary process—a full one second after Creation at a temperature of ten billion degrees—the Hadron gave birth to the electron (matter) and the positron (anti-matter).

Still later at a temperature of one billion degrees, protons and neutrons were created. Growing in abundance as the Primeval Atom expanded they formed a plasma of charged particles which, one hundred seconds after birth at a temperature of one thousand million degrees, fused together to produce one-tenth helium out of all the matter in the universe.

The helium was trapped in the primordial expanding gas, awaiting the moment when it would condense to form nebulae, galaxies, stars.

This was the Hadron Era, and with its family of psi particles determined the size and distribution of all the galaxies in the universe. Hadrons were the master templates for the ordering of matter, the DNA of Creation.

The Hadrons were something more: the first particles to possess cosmic intelligence. The universe was their creation: matter and anti-matter, time and minus time, quarks and anti-quarks. The Beginning and the End of all Creation.

Everything came from the Hadron.

1

The Discrete Charm of the Quark

MyTT had grown over the years. Funded as a co-operative research establishment by the nine planetary and five planetoidal states, it was situated on Earth IVn, within comfortable proximity—4.2 parsecs—of the Temporal Flux Centre *2U0525-06* in the inertial frame of reference Theta^2 Orionis in M.42. This meant that the round trip to and from the *Tempus* satellite Control Laboratory wouldn't greatly affect the life-spans of the technical and flight personnel—which was inevitable even though they travelled via the E.M.I. Field. The standard greeting of those returning from deep space, upon stepping down to earth, was still "God bless Oliver Heaviside," though few among them remembered that he was the nineteenth century English physicist who had first established the principle of Electro-Magnetic Interference.

The building was in the shape of a pyramid with the apex chopped off, as if a giant had taken a swipe at it with a meat cleaver, and from the flattened roof sprouted all strange manner of antenna, grouped round the opaque orange dome which housed the Black Body Radiation detection equipment. Queghan had never fathomed out why, but apparently it was necessary to compute precisely the absolute velocity of Earth IVn relative to the universe as a whole. Black Body Radiation was the universal constant, the lingering aftermath of the explosion which had created the expanding universe, and as such it could be used to relate the speed of a body passing through it.

Not that it was necessary for him to understand. Queghan wasn't a hardline scientist: he was a Myth Technologist, an occupation which straddled the Two Disciplines.

For over a year now he had been engaged on an investigation of psi particles, and in particular their relationship (if any) with the acausal nature of time, a phenomenon known in the jargon of Myth Technology as *proemptosis:* "the occurrence of an event before the calculated date." Psi particles were a family of ultra-sub-atomic constituents called quarks, a name which suited their mysterious, almost mythical existence. For did they, in fact, exist? The scientific establishment (in the manner of scientific establishments) had classified them in neat categories: red quarks, blue quarks, black quarks. They had endowed them with spurious characteristics: charm, strangeness, anti-charm and anti-strangeness. And they had proposed that they inhabited "a region of probability."

So far so good.

But the question had yet to be answered: what the hell were they? It had been shown, for example, that they had a disorienting effect on time, so could it be that time itself was not a smooth continuous motion but composed of discrete particles, the quarks, which could be isolated and identified? Matter, it had been demonstrated, consisted of nothing more substantial than a "wave motion of probability." Was time probabilistic in the same fashion? Could it be slowed down, stopped, reversed and juggled about with in the same way that quantum engineers had succeeded in tinkering with the four unified energy forces: electromagnetic, gravitational, the strong and weak nuclear interactions?

It seemed to Queghan that the universe was a question-mark. As he had once remarked to Johann Karve, Director of MyTT: "I get the feeling that somebody somewhere is having one hell of a joke at our expense. The Greatest Practical Joke Of All Time."

Karve had consoled him. "If that's so, we're all victims of the Joker, whoever he is. Nobody's party to it, Chris, that you can be sure of."

But a joke wasn't a joke unless it was shared, Queghan

felt. Where was the fun in the Joker laughing quietly to himself in some secluded corner of the universe? Unless, of course, he was mad.

The dichotomy between the Two Disciplines was never more keenly felt than when discussing the underlying purpose—for as a metaphysical science it was the task of Myth Technology to ask the elemental questions. Queghan had friends on both sides of the divide: hardliners who believed in a nuts-and-bolts universe holding itself aloft by its own bootstraps, and those others, "mystics" as they were somewhat derisively called, who were seeking the Godhead in whatever form it might choose to present itself to human consciousness. There was evidence to support both viewpoints, which was why Queghan found himself in the awkward position of agreeing and disagreeing with the two sides. It was even conceivable that both were right and both were wrong; perhaps there was no eternal all-embracing truth, simply a set of hypotheses which changed according to individual interpretation. The universe as a *fact* didn't exist—truth lay in the eyes of the observer, not in some objective reality which could be codified and classified and set down on micro-tape to rot away in Archives.

Nevertheless it was depressing, when surveying the work done over centuries since the time of Colonization, not to have arrived at a more positive conclusion. The elemental nature of spacetime was still shrouded in mystery, even though mankind had developed such concepts as the E.M.I. Field, had investigated those regions of infinite spacetime curvature, Temporal Flux Centres, known to scientists Pre-Colonization as Black Holes.

Yes, it was true, much had been achieved: the human species had been liberated from its own backyard, but it still left Queghan with the simplest and yet most complex task of all: wrestling with the enigma of those infuriating, mythical, charming quarks.

When the terra-formers had constructed Earth IVn they had given it two moons. There was no valid astrophysical or geographical reason for this, although on the planet itself it did mean that the wave barrages bordering the oceans were able to provide fifty per cent more energy output, utilizing the contra rotation and diametric opposition of the two satellites. And it gave the songwriters a rich new vein of material: *By the Light of the Silvery Moons, Blue Moons, Those Old Devil Moons,* and the latest popular hit, *How High the Moons.*

But there were other effects which hadn't been anticipated and which caused a good deal of consternation, not to say discomfort. One of these was the disruption of the female menstrual cycle. It now became clear that the 28-day ovulation period was governed by the moon of Old Earth: human evolution over millions of years had taken its cue from the motion of heavenly bodies, and the reproductive cycle was thrown into confusion by the effect of this additional gravitational force. Some women menstruated twice in the month while others ceased having a period at all. So medical science came up with the Anti-Pill to stabilize this unhappy state of affairs and once again women were able to resume their "natural" function.

This came as no real surprise to Christian Queghan, for whom Myth Technology was as much a calling as a profession. Every sub-atomic particle—the fact of its existence—affected every other particle in the universe. Subtract a single constituent, just one, and the effect on all the rest would be incalculable. It might be great or small but it would be real and, eventually, apparent.

He was a man of studious contemplation, a strange taciturn man caught up in the vortices of metaphysical speculation. The office in which he worked on Level 17 was very much like a cell, an ascetic retreat with bare walls and a slanting triangular window filled with blue sky. The warm imprint of the sun moved imperceptibly across the floor, crept into a corner, illuminated a spider's web to rainbow iridescence, and stole diagonally up the wall to the soundproof ceiling. The only items of furniture were a desk, two chairs, a bookcase, a tape library and a cyberthetic print-out terminal.

There was, too, an artefact which puzzled and intrigued

most visitors: a holograph encased in a small thermoplastic bubble which could simulate a three-dimensional representation of any person, place or thing that Queghan cared to visualize. This required intense concentration and it was an invaluable tool for keeping his gift of mythic projection in good working order. When visitors were invited to try it, all that they could manage was a ten-second burst of visual static very similar to a snowstorm; then Queghan would ask what they had hoped to see and project his interpretation of their vision. It was nothing more than a toy, albeit a useful one.

Above the door in the corridor was a warning red light. When lit it meant that the door was sealed and that Queghan was not to be disturbed under any circumstances. He was "taking a trip" as Director Karve termed it, and everyone on Level 17 was instructed to keep well away. One wag had said, "What if the complex is on fire? Do we let him burn?" and glanced slyly at the others standing nearby, and Karve had neatly wiped the smile off his face by replying, "If there is a fire Queghan will project himself back to yesterday and warn us about it, so we will prevent it happening before it starts." Nobody knew whether or not to take this as a joke; Karve seemed deadly serious.

Neither were they sure what to make of Queghan himself. To begin with, his physical appearance was . . . disturbing. He was quite tall, nearly seven feet, with broad angular shoulders that seemed out of place on his lean frame; his face had been described as "cadaverous," and his white hair and eyebrows compounded the incongruity. His age was indeterminate. A few people, close friends, knew of the mark just below the collarbone on his left shoulder: a pale discoloration of the skin in the shape of a Q. Whether it was a birthmark or a symbol of something more enigmatic—brand? stigma?—nobody knew, not even Karve. No one ever asked if Queghan himself was aware of its significance.

As with all meaningful coincidences (Queghan would have said, "Show me a coincidence that isn't acausally meaningful"), on the day that Johann Karve received the latest data from the CENTiNEL Particle Accelerator set within the Dyson Electromagnetic Sphere adjacent to *2U0525-06,* the cyberthetic terminal in Queghan's room had an attack of electronic hiccups. It was a brief malfunction but Queghan pondered on it the rest of the afternoon. He had asked for information relating to the charmed quark's rate of radioactive decay, and within seconds back came the reply:

NO REFERENCE AS SUCH. HOWEVER BY CROSS-REFERENCE INDEX CAN SUGGEST THE FOLLOWING:
(1) RATE OF SENILE DECAY FOR BOGUS MEDICAL PRACTITIONERS UNDER THE INFLUENCE OF OTHERS (ESP. OPPOSITE SEX) AS PER POPULATION MEDIAN SHOWS NO OUTSTANDING CHARACTERISTIC.
(2) QUERY RADIOACTIVE DOCTORS IN NUCLEAR WARFARE SITUATION???
(3) QUERY CHARM-ED??? CHARM-ING???
(4) EXAMPLE OF FORMER IS BOVARY/CHARLES, FICTIONAL CHARACTER OF "MADAME BOVARY", FLAUBERT/GUSTAVE, PUBLISHED 1857 (PRE-COL). EXAMPLE OF LATTER IS MORELL/THEODOR, PHYSICIAN AND CLOSE COMPANION OF HITLER/ADOLF 1936-1945 (PRE-COL).
MORE INFORMATION ON FILE RE BOTH. PLEASE ADVISE WHICH. IF THAT'S NOT ASKING TOO MUCH.

The closing remark was what passed for sardonic humour in the solid-state brain of the cyberthetic system, a machine intelligence with reasoning and deductive capability. Queghan punched back the rejoinder:

DON'T BE CHEEKY, CYB

and looked again at the print-out. What possible connection could Charles Bovary and Theodor Morell have with the rate of radioactive decay of the charmed quark? The system had queried "radioactive," though it was a common enough word in its program vocabulary, a word it used perhaps fifty times a day. He thought of calling Systems Engineering and asking them to check out the circuit, and then decided against it. Apart from the fact that the system was self-monitoring and would automatically register a malfunction, the idea of pursuing this line of inquiry, thrown up out of nowhere, intrigued him. It had to mean something: if the system felt he should be interested in a fictional character of nineteenth-century literature and Hitler's personal physician during World War II (Pre-Col), then perhaps he ought to be.

The holograph was on the desk in front of him. Queghan narrowed his concentration down to a single beam, closing mind to the outside world. His breathing became shallow, his heartbeat slowed, his neurochemical metabolism was held in stasis. Within the smooth thermoplastic sphere a series of images flickered and passed swiftly away; now and then he retained one for closer inspection, held back a fleeting impression for any significant detail it might contain—

A large airless over-furnished room. A man at his desk in sombre contemplation, gazing through the window at a distant church spire, his hands clasped in front of him in an attitude that might have been anguish or supplication. Like himself, Flaubert was in a far-away world inhabited by the phantoms of his imagination. The page in front of him on the table was half completed, the script a minuscule scrawl overlaid with a hieroglyph of additions, deletions, parentheses, arrows and question-marks. There were several other pages of manuscript scattered over the desk, some of them so heavily scored that the pen had bitten through the paper.

Queghan observed the scene, being careful not to upset the equilibrium of the image in case it revealed his presence. The writer would undoubtedly take fright at the sudden appearance of an apparition from the future, to his eyes a "ghost" materializing out of nowhere.

But there was nothing here to trigger an alarm or alert Queghan's instincts: the image had the authentic and unremarkable feel and smell of nineteenth-century France, and Flaubert too, with his perfumed hair and ink-stained fingers, fitted neatly into the tableau.

What was the cyberthetic system playing at? Queghan wondered, back once more in the bare room on Level 17. The rays of sunlight were now obscured by rags of purple cloud. He looked again at the print-out and began to smile, the heavy creases deepening at his eyes and mouth. He had been duped by his own innate gifts, for he had been seeking a dark and devious reason for the machine error when—it was now obvious—the cause was nothing more than a keyboard mistake that any trainee operator might make.

Queghan folded the print-out into the shape of a delta wing and sent it sailing across the room towards the angled window.

It was disconcerting never knowing which wife you were going home to; Queghan was duly disconcerted. This time it was the harridan.

He stepped through the front door and found himself in a hot steamy kitchen with a black-leaded range taking up the whole of one wall and an oval metal bath set before it filled with boiling water. A huge dented kettle throbbed on the cast iron hob, burbling to itself and spouting steam.

Just as his eyes were becoming accustomed to this gloomy domestic scene a hag of a woman entered the room, seeming not to notice him, and with a mumbled curse took the kettle from the hob and poured boiling water into the bath. Steam rose in clouds, enveloping her head, so that wisps of hair clung damply to her shiny forehead and sweat ran down the hollows of her scrawny neck. Her shoulders stuck out like those of a scarecrow, the drab material of her dress hanging slackly across her thin back and concave chest. She straightened up wearily and wiped her forehead with the back of her hand, catching sight of him and peering through the rising steam.

"Is that you, Paul?"

"No, this isn't Paul. It's Chris."

"Chris?" she said. "Chris?" She leaned forward, her eyes narrowed. "Where's our Paul?"

Queghan didn't want to break the spell (it would only have upset her), so he replied that Paul hadn't come home from work. He wasn't entirely sure which period this was supposed to be, though by the look of the kitchen he surmised that it was Nineteenth-Century Working Class—possibly a mining community judging by the waiting bath.

"I suppose you've come to see Paul," the hag said. "You might as well sit yourself down."

Queghan edged past the sideboard and sat down in a rocking chair whose stiff rusting springs clanged alarmingly. The period detail was good, he noted, right down to the flagstone floor and the mouse holes in the warped skirting. Now that he was included in the scenario he might as well play the part. But he wondered who Paul could be.

"Would you like some tea?" The woman had adopted a pose, the sticks of her wrists bent backwards resting on her hips, her shrewd eyes observing him keenly. There was a purple mole on her chin with a single stiff bristle growing from it.

"Yes. Thank you." He decided to reinforce the image. It would be amusing and maybe even educational. "Where's Paul working these days?"

"Nottingham," the woman said tersely, taking a pot-bellied earthenware teapot from on top of the range and pouring a thick dark-brown liquid into a mug. It looked like tea. "Bit strong," the woman said. "I mashed it ten minutes ago."

Queghan hid a smile. Good choice of phrase. Authentic dialogue. She had researched this one well. "What's Paul doing there?" He refrained from using dialect; the woman would have to accept him as an educated outsider.

"Got himself a job in an office. His father" (she pronounced it 'fae-ther') "wanted him to start down't pit but I put me foot down and said no. It might have been good enough for th'owd feller but it's not good enough for my

Paul." She placed the mug on the corner of the table, a dull spoon sticking out of it.

Queghan was watching her. He said curiously, "Your husband works in the pit?"

"Aye, that's reet," the woman said, sitting down in a straight-back chair and resting her elbows on the red and green squared oilcloth. She rubbed her eyes with prominent whitish knuckles. "Bin down't pit these twenty-odd year. Nowt better for him, never was, though there might have been once, as a young feller. Didn't take his chances. Too fond of his ale, Walter is—allus has been. Were a fine upstanding chap one time, could have charmed the birds off the trees, but it's all gone now. But I've got my Paul, he shan't ruin him, I'll see to that." Quite unexpectedly she started to cry. Her eyes appeared to be dry and yet the tears ran down and plopped on the oilcloth. She sniffled into a rag of a handkerchief and said, "Good heavens, drink your tea now, pay no attention to me."

Queghan was embarrassed to be near such emotion, even though he knew it to be fabricated in the same way as the flagstone floor, the mouse holes, the creaking rocking chair, the thin bleached knuckles. . .

And something else was troubling him. The scene had the nagging familiarity of a half-remembered dream, of something experienced long ago, or depicted on the screen, or read about. Of course he had seen details of the period before—the frugal surroundings, the hardships, the raw nerve of living on the poverty line—yet somehow she had caught not merely a similitude of the environment and the conditions but a specific human situation at a certain time and place.

This wasn't, Queghan felt, the enactment of just another historical reconstruction, an amusing diversion: it was nearer to the nub of things, closer to some underlying truth than a clever replication of period detail.

He said, "Don't upset yourself. I'm sure that what you're doing is for the best. Your husband will understand."

The woman blew her nose and sniffed her tears away. She smiled at him. "What must you think of me, weeping in front of a stranger? You mustn't mention this to Paul, he'd be angry with me. He says tears should only be used for happiness, not for sorrow."

"You love your son very much," Queghan said.

"I live for him," the woman said simply. "He is my life."

"He's very fortunate to have someone like you."

The woman tossed her head and laughed, a little harshly. "You try telling *him* that. He thinks I interfere too much in his affairs. He's very stubborn. I say, 'You don't have the experience, you're very young, Paul,' but he thinks he knows best. The girl at the farm, she's turned his head, filled him up with ideas. But whenever I warn him he says, 'I can look after myself, mother. No girl will ever come between us. I watch them. I see their little snares and wiles; they won't trap me. Never.' But he's so young, he doesn't know about life. He doesn't understand women."

"And what about the one in Nottingham?" Queghan said.

The woman reacted sharply. Her hands went together and clasped themselves in a knot on the oilcloth, the pale bones showing. "Who told you about her?" Her brows were drawn into fierce, rigid lines. "Is it common knowledge?"

"Rumour," Queghan admitted cautiously. "People talk, and something like that is bound to get around. A married woman and a younger man."

"They do talk," the woman said, barely controlling herself. "That's all some of them can do, talk." She closed her eyes wearily and shook her head from side to side. "I've warned him, begged him to be more careful." She opened her eyes and looked at him directly. "Of course it's her that's to blame. These women nowadays, these so-called modern women, they have no shame. They're nothing more than brazen—" She fumbled for a word to express her meaning without offending him. "Trollops."

"It's the times," Queghan said placatingly.

"Aye, the times," the woman agreed sourly. "The times change but folk remain the same. One of these days he'll learn. One of these days—" She held up a scrawny hand. "Hush!"

Queghan heard nothing.

"Sit quiet," the woman said, getting up herself. "It's

Morel. He's been in the pub swilling himself stupid with ale as usual. Sit quiet and he'll pay you no mind." She stood at the table, listening intently to the perfect silence, and suddenly her hand went up and clutched the faded dress above her heart. Her face was ashen.

"Are you ill?" Queghan said, anxious despite himself.

She shook her head, unable to speak for the moment. Then she moistened her pale lips; her gaze steadied and sought him out. "I'm all right," she murmured. "Don't say anything. I'm all right."

"You ought to see a doctor."

"Doctors." The woman tried a smile but it was twisted and full of pain. "Wouldn't give 'em house room. Quacks most of them. Keep you ill so's they can take your money. That's the only thing we agree on, Morel and me." Once again she fell silent and her eyes seemed to withdraw as if observing an inner landscape: a private fantasy world locked inside her head.

She stood at the table, her hands suspended in mid-gesture, as still and unyielding as a waxwork. Queghan got up and left the kitchen; she didn't see him go even though he crossed her eye-line and passed by close enough to touch.

Something that Karve always said came to him now: "Ignore a coincidence at your peril," and Queghan now had two separate events to contend with within the space of a few hours. Something somewhere was juggling with the incidence of probability, manipulating spacetime and causing it to distort.

These "coincidences" were the peaks of waves which his senses could detect but not so far comprehend. And the odd thing was that they were in some way connected with his search for the mysterious psi particles which constituted the basic stuff of time and matter.

The quarks were coming home to roost.

At dinner he asked his wife why she had chosen a scene from *Sons and Lovers* and she looked at him blankly for a moment and then shook her head. She was wearing an emerald-green velvet evening gown, gathered and held at her breast by a gold pin, her shoulders bare and gently contoured in the lamplight, soft dark recesses nestling above her collar-bones. The fine curve of her neck was emphasized by the smooth blond hair swept back above her ears which gleamed like old silver in the mellow light.

Queghan suggested to her that there must have been a reason. "Was it specified as an educational project?"

"I didn't intend making it a fictional scene," Oria said. "It was simply an accurate historical reconstruction." Her eyes shifted momentarily and became vague. For some time she had been unwell.

"I couldn't fault its accuracy—I could even smell the coal dust. But you introduced fictional characters, Paul, Morel, the Nottingham woman."

"But I didn't," Oria said. Her delicate hands moved like slender pale fish in the lamplight. "All I had in mind was to capture authentic period detail. The characters must have imposed themselves . . . I don't know how or why."

Queghan drank some wine. He smiled and said, "I wish you'd warned me. Finding your wife made up as a hag isn't the best sort of homecoming."

"I lost track of time. I'm sorry, Chris. And I didn't expect you for at least another hour." She smiled uncertainly. "I shouldn't keep doing this, I know."

"A harmless fantasy never hurt anybody."

Oria nodded. She wasn't entirely certain that any fantasy was totally harmless. Later in the evening they listened to classical tribal music. Oria was restless and she became annoyed with Queghan because he didn't respond to her attempts to make conversation. In a way she didn't understand, this rather pleased her, though she still put on a show of irritation—the truth being that it pleased her when his mind drifted away in abstract speculation, excluding her and everything else; it was a trait which endeared him to her even as her feminine pride was snubbed. Had he always been attentive she wouldn't have loved him so much.

"But I do," Queghan said, smiling faintly. "I do listen to you."

"Perhaps if I took a lover you might be more considerate."

"Which period did you have in mind? English Regency? Greek Bacchanalia? Maybe something modern, post-Colonization?"

"I didn't mean a reconstruction," Oria said tartly. "I meant live-action experience. You remember—real life?"

"That's the stuff between the scenes?"

"Why did I marry you?" Oria said. "You come back from the nether world like a whale surfacing for a breath of air. Then down again into the deep."

"You've never seen a whale."

"My grannie told me all about them."

"Your grannie never saw a whale. We don't have whales. They forgot to bring the embryos. We have blowfish instead, the size of office blocks."

"What have blowfish the size of office blocks to do with my taking a lover?"

"You could take a blowfish for a lover."

"That's an obscene suggestion, not to say physically awkward and cumbersome in bed."

"Could be a lot of fun."

"Who for?"

"The blowfish."

Oria leaned closer. The demarcation between green velvet and white breast was very evident. She said:

"Let's try another ploy. Blowfish aren't sexy."

"They are to other blowfish."

Oria started giggling. "Stop it, Chris." She reached out and stroked his cheek.

"Which ploy is this?" Queghan asked, giving her a sidelong look. But it had been too near the truth to be comfortable and Oria snatched her hand away. She was very beautiful, still desirable, and it was a pity they had to play at games to touch reality. It was necessary to simulate the correct responses.

How long since a human being had responded spontaneously and involuntarily to stimuli? There had been an overkill of emotion and the human species had grown weary, like an actor forced to play a role until it became a mumbled ritual, empty of meaning, devoid of feeling.

Now Oria had taken on her affronted virgin pose. She had offered herself and been rejected: the young and tender innocent spurned and cast aside. The trouble with the image was that she was thirty-nine years old and had a son of seventeen.

Queghan said, "I'm too tired to play. Let's go to bed."

She looked warily at him and said, "I'm tired as well."

"Really tired?"

"Actually tired."

"I think we've established that we're both tired," and he smiled into her grey-green eyes. Behind those eyes there was a universe he knew nothing about. He supposed that in some ways it corresponded to his own, that there were certain points of similarity. But to know for sure he would have to enter her mind, and so far he had only succeeded in penetrating her body.

Queghan bent forward to kiss her, wondering what he ought to feel and what his response should be.

2

RECONPAN

Johann Karve had spent a restless night. As a rule he slept soundly, untroubled by whatever cares the day had heaped upon his ageing shoulders; but the latest results from the CENTiNEL Particle Accelerator had been more than merely disturbing, they had been alarming.

He sat at his desk on Level 40 of MyTT drinking lukewarm tea from a china cup, turning the pages of research data: column after column of nine-digit numbers which varied only by the last two, in some cases the last three, decimal places. These were the reassuring ones. But here and there amongst the endless rows of grey figures a red asterisk shrilled a warning like a beacon on a foggy night. His first and natural conclusion, after observing these maverick numbers, had been "cyberthetic malfunction." It was the obvious explanation, the calming shot which numbed the shock to the sensory nerve system and intellectual processes. Or failing that explanation (and it had died a miserable death on reading the addendum to the report which stated that the data had been independently verified) one could always suppose that the Particle Accelerator itself had detected a freak interaction of mu-meson particles in the region of the Temporal Flux Centre *2U0525-06*. After all, it was an unusual region of spacetime where time dilation was at optimum.

Yet even this would not do. As Director of the Myth Technology Research Institute he had to rely on the expertise of hardline scientists, but he was not such a fool that he couldn't read a particle accelerator report and interpret the findings in a meaningful fashion. The decay rate of mu-mesons was precisely calibrated: cyberthetic analysis had already allowed for the fact that they lived seven times longer than was theoretically possible. Created by the collision between energetic protons emanating from super-nova explosions elsewhere in the galaxy, their very high speeds—a fraction below lightspeed—enabled them to age slower than other particles in the same spatio-temporal co-ordinate.

And not only were the mu-mesons behaving strangely. The really worrying aspect was that a whole range of elementary psi particles, companions of the neutron and proton, denoted Σ, Λ, Ξ and so on, had suddenly taken it into their heads to alter their rates of decay. If time dilation wasn't the culprit this left only one possibility, but it was the one Karve was reluctant to accept.

In simple terms it meant that the fabric of spacetime was disintegrating.

The atomic structure of elementary particles, which constituted the stuff of energy and matter, was behaving erratically and breaking all the rules of physics. The figures in front of him were evidence of this—these ordered grey columns which foretold that organic structure, and time itself, were breaking down. There would be no cataclysmic explosion, no supra-galactic event to signal the end of time—merely the creeping infinitesimal process of disintegration and decay.

And how would this process announce itself? Karve picked up the china cup and supported it lightly by the outspread tips of his fingers. Inside this "dead" piece of matter a thousand billion billion particles were busily humming away in their orbits: atoms within molecules; electrons, protons and neutrons within atoms; and within these subatomic particles the infinitely smaller constituent parts which were the wave-forms of pure energy. Nothing very dramatic was required to make this whole elaborate structure crumble into nothingness, to dissipate itself in a burst of radiation. True, the amount of radiation generated would be enough to devastate an area several kilometres square, but essentially the atomic structure would simply have to break the rules and stop behaving as it had done since the formation of the primeval atom all those thousands of millions of years ago.

Then—nothing.

The cup would cease to exist. The atomic structure which obligingly kept to the shape of a cup for the purpose of drinking tea would quite arbitrarily decide to take on some other formation, or perhaps not to assume a definite pattern at all. Chaos would rule. Particles would interact at random in a formless plasma of non-matter. Or perhaps entropy would come, once and for evermore, to hold the universe in a state of lukewarm apathy. The ultimate heat death in which everything stayed where it was because it couldn't be bothered to go anywhere else. In the absence of matter and energy interchange, communication would cease. Lightspeed would become a meaningless and futile concept. Spacetime would be defunct. And without these universal ground rules time itself would stop. Dead.

Karve believed intellectually in the probability, if not the actual possibility, of these thoughts; he was too much the scientist to refute them and turn his face away in blind obstinacy. Intellectually yes, they could happen, but emotionally his own senses rebelled against the dogma of clinical scientific objectivity. The *feel* of the cup touching his fingertips could not be measured by any device known to man. The sense of well-being he experienced from the broad shaft of sunlight warming his hand, and the memories it evoked of other sunfilled days, could not be contained in a scientific treatise or marked by the indices on a Gaussian curve. Even looking out, as he did each day, from the apex of the pyramid, imbued his whole being with the inexpressible wonder of vibrant life so that the entire body of human knowledge lay in its shadow. The fact of existence, the mystery of creation, were still the abiding and elemental truths.

The sheets of figures, the innumerable grey columns, called him back to duty. He was an old man, his days of innovation and creativity long past. His brain was now the repository of a million facts, a human card index lacking the spark of synthesis which was the basis of scientific inquiry.

Only connect, he thought. The answer was that simple.

His First Assistant came through on audio. Karve listened patiently but yet with a trace of weariness to some meandering second-hand complaint from RECONPAN. It had been filed by deGrenier, who had insisted on a personal interview with the Director.

"I would have thought," Karve told his First Assistant, "that Systems Engineering or perhaps Archives could have settled this to everyone's satisfaction." The two areas he most dreaded becoming involved with, and this particular problem combined them: hardware and administration.

"DeGrenier has taken the matter up with both sections, sir, and neither can offer an adequate explanation." The First Assistant paused, and then like a mother hoping to reason with a recalcitrant child: "I think under the circumstances it might be wise. . ."

Karve pushed the CENTiNEL report to one side. "Send deGrenier in," he said, and while he waited studied the china cup and saucer on the desk as if expecting them to dematerialize before his eyes.

DeGrenier was brisk, businesslike and to the point.

"I'm sorry to take up your time, Director, but somebody has been tampering with the information retrieval system. Yesterday I requested biographical details to build up a Subject Profile and this is what came up."

Karve took the yellow print-out, comprising several sheets folded concertina fashion. He read:

> RATE OF DECAY AS PER UPDATED CENTiNEL REPORT (REF 29-1493b/0012) IN ACCORDANCE WITH MASTER FILE (HEAD QUARK/SUB ANTI/SUB CHARM/SUB STRANGE) WITH THE FOLLOWING ADDITIONS, DELETIONS AND AMENDMENTS:

Then followed row upon row of symbols and figures, several thousand of them neatly tabulated in blocks of electric type.

"I take it that these aren't the biographical details you were after," Karve said dryly, glancing up at deGrenier.

"No, they are not. May I sit down?"

"I'm sorry," Karve said. "Please. How rude of me. Would you care for some tea?"

"No, thank you," deGrenier said stiffly.

These hardliners, Karve thought. Nothing must stand in their way. A screw strips its thread and they have a nervous breakdown. Though that wasn't entirely fair, he chided himself; deGrenier was a gifted and dedicated scientist who virtually single-handed had developed the RECONPAN project from a feasibility study to the point where it was a practical research technique. It wouldn't be too long before operational trials were under way. The Director had never been absolutely sure how RECONPAN functioned or what its specific purpose was supposed to be. No doubt it would be useful for something.

"This kind of thing is most disruptive," deGrenier said portentously. "We're already behind schedule and to have some fool tampering with vital information. . ."

Karve smiled in his gentle myopic way. This image of bumbling academic was a subterfuge he had brought to a fine level of accomplishment. "Are you suggesting that someone is deliberately falsifying information?" he said, his tangled grey eyebrows forming a line of undergrowth above his polarized bifocals.

"Well, perhaps not deliberately," deGrenier amended.

"You used the word 'tampering' which implies an act of wilful malpractice. Or a practical joke."

"I take a dim view of practical jokes."

"It seems to me that either it's a system malfunction or human error. I shall have to find out who or what is responsible. I'm sorry if your work has been impaired in any way." He smiled his gentle lingering smile.

"I had to wait hours for that information and when it arrived it was worse than useless. Pages of meaningless figures."

"Meaningless?" the Director said. "Not to someone working in the field of study relating to quarks. There are other projects here in addition to RECONPAN."

It was the nearest Karve could bring himself to an outright rebuke. As deGrenier stood up he said: "Whose biographical details were you seeking?" And holding the print-out aloft: "In place of this meaningless jumble?"

"Theodor Morell, German National, round about the period 1936 to 1945 Pre-Colonization."

"Not a name familiar to me."

"Rather unlikely unless you'd made a special study of the mid-Twentieth, in particular the Second World War. Morell was a top Nazi physician. Not a great deal is known about him and I was hoping to fill in the background. Instead I received the life history and mating habits of the mythical quark."

It was the first time he had known deGrenier make a remark that was intended to be humorous. His curiosity was aroused. He said, "Was Morell qualified? I mean, was he a good doctor?"

"The evidence so far, what little we have, would suggest not," deGrenier said, pausing by the door. "He sometimes used drugs without knowing what effect they would have, experimenting on his patients and giving massive overdoses."

"I see." Karve was looking over his bifocals at deGrenier's legs. They were rather nice legs. The scientist seemed unaware of this flattering scrutiny, though she might not have considered it all that flattering, coming from the Director of the Institute, a man more than twice her age.

"So it would be fair to describe him as a quack."

"I suppose so," deGrenier said indifferently.

"That might explain one or two things."

"Might it?"

Karve nodded slowly and dropped the print-out on the desk. "I'll see that this finds its rightful owner."

"Thank you, Director." Her face had relaxed into a tentative smile. It was quite rare for Pouline deGrenier. She went out.

Yet another reason for being alive, Karve thought, the

pleasure a beautiful woman could bestow simply by her presence. It wasn't healthy for a man of his age to have such notions. The desire would be awakened but not appeased, and his casual appraisal of her legs might have led to other fanciful flights of imagination which old men were supposed to have outgrown—as if advancing years killed the urge completely. They did not, of course, merely the opportunity.

Karve reached out to take the cup from its saucer and as he did so the handle came away and the cup smashed itself into dozens of tiny fragments, too many and too small to count.

Queghan waited philosophically for the third coincidence.

He was not by nature a patient man but he had taught himself to curb his restlessness, knowing that the harder he sought the third coincidence the further it would recede. The only way to snare it was by allowing it to catch him.

The print-out arrived in his room on Level 17 with a note attached, which read: "Gremlins at work again. Or would it be more accurate to say a quirk in the system?" and it was signed "Johann".

Karve had evidently made the right connection. But as one of the founders of the metaphysical science known as Myth Technology his working hypothesis for life was based on the principle of acausal relationships. No two events were necessarily connected in direct sequence, though the connection was there if you knew how and where to look. In his book *The Hidden Universe* Karve had referred to these connections as "the leys"—intangible filaments of meaning which held everything together: man, matter, energy, space, time.

Queghan detached the note and underneath it was the triangular stamp with which each Section identified the material in its possession. Inside the triangle the word RECONPAN followed by the initials "P. deG" and the date of receipt.

Why had Pouline deGrenier received the information pertaining to HEAD QUARK/SUB ANTI/SUB CHARM/SUB STRANGE? Was it that the cyberthetic system had got its wires crossed? But the system was supposedly proof against errors of that kind, self-programmed to detect and rectify them.

Now supposing, Queghan thought, indulging in his favorite pastime, supposing the information relating to the quarks was in some way pertinent to the RECONPAN project but that Pouline deGrenier had failed to make the connection. It would possibly mean that the cyberthetic system (or something guiding the system) was pointing them in the direction they didn't realize was the correct one—rather like a guide dog leading a blind man away from a precipice he doesn't know is there.

Supposing, too, that the same applied in his case. He had asked for information on the decay rate of quarks and been offered instead a fictional character called Charles Bovary and an obscure doctor who had something to do with the Hitler movement on Old Earth.

And supposing he was just chasing rainbows. Maybe a micro-circuit had flipped its lid and everyone in the building was receiving cuckoo information. Some suppositions, unfortunately, had the leaden ring of cracked bells.

Queghan pressed the ALERT tab on the input terminal and sat back as the lights started to blink and the machine hummed to itself. He had a love-hate relationship with the cyberthetic box of tricks, and it wouldn't have surprised him to know it felt the same; they were old sparring partners.

After several moments had elapsed the system said: *Can I be of service?* Evidently tired of waiting.

"I'm perplexed."

The human condition, so I'm told.

"I can do without the homespun philosophy."

I've just been oiled.

"And the cyberthetic wit."

Sorry. Do you need me or are you just passing the time of day?

"How's your memory of the Second World War Pre-Colonization?" Queghan asked.

There was a slight, though significant, pause.

Comprehensive.

"It isn't on your mind? I mean obsessively."

I'm not programmed for obsessions.

"Aren't you the lucky one."

That's a matter of opinion.

"You gave me some incorrect information yesterday, Cyb."

Not possible. If it was incorrect there must have been an error at the input terminal. I have registered no malfunction in the past twenty-four hours.

"That's your discreet cyberthetic way of saying that I punched in the wrong question."

I am stating a fact. No malfunction occurred.

Queghan took out a pack of Nexus-T. He extracted one of the coloured plastic tubes and inhaled deeply. His senses seemed to vibrate in the fumes. He said:

"What do you know about RECONPAN?"

Had the cyberthetic system been programmed to sigh it might have done so. *A lot,* it said.

"Is it classified?"

Yes. Do you require the security reference?

Queghan released purple fumes into the still air. They ascended to the ceiling in a hazy spiral. As a mythographer he had clearance on all projects within MyTT, classified or not. The system was humouring him. He let a few seconds go by, just to show which of them was the human being.

"Do you find Pouline deGrenier attractive?" he said at last.

I know what attractiveness means but I don't comprehend it. You mustn't play semantic games with me, Queghan, it isn't fair.

"You've been playing games with me."

Not true, the cyberthetic system protested. It sounded almost hurt. A machine with offended feelings.

Queghan said, "Is RECONPAN anywhere near operational?"

One moment. The system went away and delved into the depths of its billionfold cellular memory. There was a muted beep and then: *Experimental trials are scheduled but they are having difficulty with the tissue cultures which are not retaining the neurons as expected. Reconstruction of the Subject's memory file is as per classification in—*

"Never mind the classification. As I recall, and you can correct me if I'm wrong, RECONPAN is the reconstruction of a human brainpan."

Correct.

"How is this achieved?"

By complete analysis and correlation of all material in Archives; everything written or known or recorded about the Subject—letters, books, speeches, newstapes, sound recordings, contemporary accounts and documents—every known fact is processed and a neurological simulation of the Subject's brainpan is constructed in the laboratory. The current difficulty is due to Psycho-Med being unable to stimulate self-generation of tissue cultures.

"Explain."

The brain functions but is not technically alive. In order to achieve operational capability the tissue cultures must be capable of generating and transmitting neurochemical data.

"And they haven't managed to do this."

No.

Queghan took the fumes into his lungs and the room seemed to shimmer as the drug distorted the parallax of reality.

"Have they chosen the Subject for the experimental trials?"

Yes.

"Who is it?"

Adolf Schicklgruber by birth, later known as Adolf Hitler. German National, early Twentieth Pre-Colonization. Austrian by birth, became German Chancellor in—

"Thank you, Cyb," Queghan interrupted gently. "I do know who Adolf Hitler was."

If there was any dissension at MyTT it usually revolved round Johann Karve's original dictum that the proper field of study was the interpretation of past and future myths. This statement of the Institute's primary aim had sparked off a continuing debate which occasionally flared into open confrontation.

Karve proposed that myths and legends were repositories of knowledge—"centres of human consciousness in which we find certain intuitive and elemental truths" in his phrase. As a useful analogy he often compared them to the eye of a hurricane, the dead-still centre of a vortex where nothing takes place but around which a mad whirl of activity is going on. "Imagine time as a vortex," he said in his lectures, "rushing around in a frenzy of apparently meaningless and random interactions. Time is composed of events, in our case events on a human scale which mark off the passing years, and now and then these events coagulate at a particular spatio-temporal co-ordinate. This is what we call a myth. Now if we can analyse myths and interpret them correctly we shall gain an insight into the underlying meaning and purpose of the Metagalaxy—an eye into the elemental nature of time."

Those on the mystical or metaphysical side of the Two Disciplines could accept this readily enough, but for those on the other, more concerned with the practical development and application of advanced technology, these were concepts not easily grasped or gratefully received.

As a hardline scientist working in Myth Technology Pouline deGrenier tried to embrace, somewhat awkwardly, the two extremes. It was a contradiction she was not unaware of. In private conversation with Léon Steele, her Third Assistant, she sometimes referred to her "schizophrenic position" in the Institute, of being neither fish nor fowl.

Steele was a young man of nervous disposition. He had once thought himself to be (perhaps he still was) in love with Pouline deGrenier. He had assisted her on the RECONPAN project for over a year and their relationship had been cordial until the sweating grunting struggle had taken place in a dusty subsection of Archives (HEAD WAR/SUB PRE-COL/SUB WORLD II) and his ardour had gone off the boil. Since then he had tried, with a fair measure of success, to play the role of the intense, dedicated professional researcher.

The trouble with this was that he found her physically unbearable to be near without being able to touch: his calm and rational self told him not to be such a fool while the rest of him lusted after her like a child in front of a confectionery display. Though he still insisted to himself that he was definitely, emphatically, categorically not in love with her.

This didn't prevent him from offering her a few minutes of rather fawning sympathy: "The Director is out of touch," he agreed. "What else can you expect of an old man?"

"The establishment is going downhill. How can we get on with our work if the systems we rely on, and in particular the information retrieval circuit, are not functioning properly? He smiled. The man actually smiled as though the problem was unimportant. It wouldn't surprise me—it really *wouldn't* surprise me if he doesn't know what the RECONPAN project is all about. You're right, he's too old; out of touch—"

That cold briskness in her voice, she hated it. It sounded in her ears like the voice of someone she wouldn't wish to know. It had an unpleasant grating quality, lacking all trace of emotion.

Léon had the annoying habit of pulling at his finger joints whenever he was listening to anyone, and now he nodded his head sympathetically to the accompaniment of clicking bone.

"Please don't do that. It goes right through me."

"What?" Léon said, startled.

"Whatever it is you do with your fingers."

Léon looked down at his empty hands, frowning.

"Come along, we're wasting time."

"Oh yes," Léon said. He suddenly remembered: "Miss Ritblat in Psycho-Med has been trying to reach you." He faltered. "I'm sorry, I should have told you before."

Pouline deGrenier never liked speaking to Karla Ritblat, head of the Psycho-Med Faculty, though she had little choice in the matter. The other woman was rigid to the point of being cyberthetic, straight-backed and thin-lipped with a helmet of silver hair: it was Pouline deGrenier thirty years hence—or how she feared she might become if some man didn't come along and claim her. She had her career sure enough, and it was fulfilling, but the essential core of her life seemed to be dribbling inconsequentially away. She felt herself to be in shadow, on the edge of a bright light, never at the true centre of things.

"I think we're making progress." Karla Ritblat said when they had made contact. Neither woman bothered with the viewing panel. "The cultures are responding to cobalt-7 radiation: we've only tried it in short low-intensity bursts for fear of causing damage to the DNA structure. But the results so far are promising."

"How soon will you know if the cultures are able to accept neurochemical data?"

"We mustn't run before we can walk," said Karla Ritblat. A gentle admonishment from the headmistress to the pupil teacher. Pouline felt herself flushing. She breathed evenly and said:

"I shall require a time-scale projection for the next three months to co-ordinate your efforts with ours. The Subject Profile is almost completed."

"You'll need a lot of information to fill one hundred billion neuron cells."

"I think we have enough," Pouline deGrenier responded crisply. "Everything now depends on the tissue cultures, if and when they're available." That was one in the eye for Karla Ritblat.

She broke contact to forestall any further allusive comment and became aware that someone was standing at the door to the office. She took in several confused impressions all at once: slender height, the peculiar rake of the shoulders, a lean gaunt face heavily creased near the nostrils and mouth, white hair cropped short. It was the mythographer Queghan, whom she knew by reputation but had never spoken to or seen at such close quarters.

Her body chemistry was upset: part fear, part fascination.

"I passed your assistant on the way in. He said it would be all right. If you're busy—"

"No. Of course. Come in. Sit down." (Why, Pouline wondered, was she speaking so idiotically, like somebody with a wooden jaw?)

She was thankful when he sat down; his height had been forbidding. He introduced himself, adding that he worked as a mythographer on Level 17. She was thinking furiously what possible reason he could have for coming to see her, and at the same time taking in his strange appearance. She noticed his hands in particular and saw that the nails were pale elongated ovals, almost transparent. She thought, An odd fish.

He began: "I don't know too much about the RECONPAN project beyond a potted briefing from the cyberthetic system, but yesterday rather a curious thing happened. Your Section and mine were juxtaposed at a certain world point."

"How interesting," Pouline said tamely. "At least it would be if I knew what that meant."

"Forgive me, I have this nasty habit of using jargon. I meant there was a coincidence involving our two Sections; some information which went astray."

"Ah yes," Pouline said, none too kindly. "So you were the one. There was indeed a mix-up on the information retrieval circuit—either that or somebody had been tampering with the cyberthetic system." There was a veiled accusation there somewhere.

"Possibly." He hadn't spotted the inference or else had chosen to ignore it.

"What else could it be?"

Queghan held up his hand and ticked the points off on his long fingers. "One: the system reported no malfunction within the past twenty-four hours. Two: neither of us received the information we had requested. Three: on the same day you asked for information on Theodor Morell there was a keyboard error and up came Morell's name on the print-out. The odds against that happening by accident are several billion to one. I haven't computed the exact ratio."

Pouline shook her head, slightly baffled. "All that went

wrong, surely, is that I received your information and you received mine. Isn't that what happened?"

"No, it isn't. I never asked for the information you received. By mistake I punched in the word 'quack' instead of 'quark', a one-letter substitution, and the system came up with the nearest approximation to 'a charming quack'. But then you received information on the decay rate of quarks which, it so happened, I hadn't asked for."

By now Pouline was totally lost. She nodded slowly, trying to make sense of it and thinking what a strange colour Queghan's eyes were, neither brown nor blue or—

"And there could be another mystery."

"Which is?"

"What became of *your* information? I'm assuming you asked for details of Morell. But you didn't receive them and neither did I."

"I asked for biographical details to build up a Subject Profile, that's true. But if there wasn't an interchange of information how would you know that? Did the Director mention it?"

Queghan smiled suddenly and quite charmingly: it came as a surprise that his austere face was capable of such mercurial change. "It was the only illogical explanation."

"Do you base all your assumptions on illogical premises?" she asked. It annoyed her that he seemed to be enjoying a private joke at her expense.

"I thrive on them," he said, still smiling.

"It doesn't get us very far."

Queghan conceded the truth of this. "If we could discover what happened to the Morell biography it might give us a clue."

"I don't have time to indulge in detective stories."

"Or perhaps it was deliberately suppressed."

It was Pouline's turn to smile, though it was more cynical than amused. "By the cyberthetic system?"

"That had occurred to me as a possibility. But as you know the system is self-programmed to prevent incorrect or misleading information coming into circulation. I don't think the system is at fault."

It wasn't, Pouline realized, only his physical appearance which disturbed her. There was something else. She realized with a swift disquieting shock what it was: he was able to see into her mind. It was as though she was naked in front of him, an affront to the senses that made a cold creeping sickness reach up and envelop her, the taste of iron in her mouth. With an effort of will she said:

"I fail to see the point of this. Some information has gone astray. It isn't the first time and it won't be the last."

"Aren't you curious? And what about the information you received—that wasn't even requested?"

"I can't explain it."

"Neither can I and it worries me. Or I should say that I can think of an explanation but I don't understand it." He laced his fingers together and sat staring at her. Pouline shifted uncomfortably; it was hateful to be scrutinized like this.

Queghan said presently, "Supposing there is a connection between the RECONPAN project and my investigation of quark and anti-quark particles."

"Not possible," Pouline said shortly.

"There is a theory," he went on, "that alongside our own universe, existing side by side with it, there is a universe made up of anti-quarks. An anti-quark universe. It could be here with us now, at this moment in time, occupying the same spatio-temporal co-ordinate—the only difference being that its basic sub-atomic constituents are anti-quarks existing in minus time."

"Then we should be able to detect it," Pouline deGrenier said, ever the pragmatic hardliner.

"Perhaps we can. We can't detect it with our scientific instruments because they can only operate in our own universe. But imagine for a moment that in place of eyes and ears human beings were equipped with X-ray and infra-red sensory equipment. We should see a different kind of universe altogether. The sea and sky would no longer be blue. Solid objects would appear to be transparent. We should be able to hear the stars. We can only picture the universe as it appears to our own limited senses."

"I know all this," Pouline deGrenier said icily. "I did a two-year postgraduate course in electromagnetic wave theory."

"Then you should have no difficulty grasping the concept of an anti-quark universe existing alongside our own."

"We have no proof that it does."

"We have no proof that it doesn't."

"Very well. Let's say I accept the possibility of what you say. Where does it take us?"

"To the consideration of another possibility: that some unspecified agency has engineered all this."

"Engineered?"

"The clues have been laid—unless, that is, we're too blind to see them. Something is operating in a stratum of spacetime which normally would be invisible to our senses. Deliberately or accidentally, I don't know which, it has made its presence known to us."

Pouline gazed at him. Her features had hardened into a frown. She said, "What has any of this to do with RECONPAN? Or with Morell? It's sheer nonsense. The project is solely concerned with neurochemical reconstruction of brain cells, with the simulation of the Subject's brain."

"That's right," Queghan said. "And we shouldn't forget the Subject you've chosen for experimental trials."

Pouline looked into those peculiar eyes of his, transfixed by his gaze, and the silence hung in the air between them.

3

The Diaries of Dr. Morell

Berlin, July 1938
The trees looked lovely this morning as I walked along the Wilhelmstrasse on my way to the Chancellery. The city gardeners perform an excellent service in keeping the place neat and trim and shipshape. It was a pleasure to be abroad and on such a fine morning.

A tedious incident which took the edge off my good humour and benign disposition: one of the guards, presumably new on the duty roster, stood in my way and asked to see my papers. He obviously didn't know who I was and remained obdurate when I informed him that I was a member of the Sanctum.

"Papers," he insisted, barring my way.

I repeated my name, laying emphasis on the *Doktor,* and added that I was Leibarzt to the Führer. He looked rather startled at this, but the buffoon had been given strict instructions and was determined to carry them out to the letter.

When I had presented my papers he went rigidly to attention, his eyes frozen and dead like those of a statue. I told him that if he ever stopped me again, for any reason whatsoever, it would be the worse for him. I think we parted in mutual understanding.

The days pass hectically but none the less pleasantly. There is much activity all around—political activity I refer to—which imbues the whole place with a sense of urgency and purpose. Three new departments have been set up in the past month and there are clerks scurrying everywhere carrying files and memoranda and bits of paper. I enjoy the comings and goings precisely because I am detached from them, an observer rather than a participant—though it is difficult at times *not* to become involved. However, I follow my own course, quietly and without attracting attention: the time will come when moves have to be made and decisions taken. For the moment I am content to wait.

One advantage of this detachment is the overall view it gives me of those closest to the seat of power and their assorted jockeying for favour and position. I have marked out Bormann as being one of those who will repay close attention and careful study: he is quiet, unobtrusive, but I have noticed in conference that he is ever-watchful, missing nothing with those dark shrewd eyes of his. In particular he watches Himmler, alert to his every political ploy, though it has to be said that the two of them get on well together—that is, they show all the signs of being on close, friendly terms, often dining together and patronizing the same whorehouse.

Of the rest it is hard to choose who would win the award of Prize Idiot at the annual Chancellery ball. They posture about the place, seeking to outdo the others with the splendor of their uniforms and the size of their bodyguards. New notices go up almost every day directing one to this or that new department, the theory being, I suppose, that importance, prestige and power are in direct proportion to the volume of paperwork any one department can manufacture. The more departments, the greater the avalanche of useless confetti.

The only member of the Sanctum I should disassociate from this observation is Reichsminister Goebbels, head of Information and Propaganda, whose visits to the Führer are businesslike and without the ostentatious foolery of motorcycle escorts and fleets of cars and stamping salutes. He is a small, slim, dark-haired man, quietly-spoken, with a lean ascetic countenance. On the numerous occasions when I have been in conference with him he has always displayed an astute intelligence, a ready grasp of essentials, and occasionally a droll sense of humour, very welcome, which completely goes over the heads of the other dolts.

A good man to have on your side, I would have thought: loyal, a keen mind, well organized, and not one to suffer fools gladly, if at all.

My duties are not arduous but I think it wise to keep up the pretence of being fully involved and hard at work; it is easy enough to do: ordering supplies from the Clinic in the Ziegelstrasse, circulating minor queries to and fro between myself, Brandt and von Hasselbach, inspecting the medical orderlies and making sure they have enough adhesive plaster and clean bandages, supervising the Führer's meals and rest periods. He has been liverish for the past couple of days and I managed to obtain a large consignment (six gross packs each containing 100 tablets) of that old standby remedy Dr. Koester's Antigas Pills, a compound of strychnine and belladonna. Two tablets after each meal, eight daily, seemed to do the trick. He is much settled.

I heard from my cousin Felix yesterday about our joint scheme to manufacture the nerve tonic. Felix has taken out a lease on some premises in Budapest and is already advertising for a small labour force of women to start production later this year. It was fortuitous to come across the complete description of the tonic (including chemical formula) in an American medical journal. One minor problem, as Felix has pointed out, is that some of the ingredients are difficult to come by and rather expensive, so I have written back recommending certain cheap substitutes which are easily obtained in bulk. The effects shouldn't be all that different; and in any case it's difficult to tell with nerve complaints whether or not an improvement has been made.

I spoke to Elisabeth Schroeder, one of the Führer's private secretaries (charming creature!) and we discussed the forthcoming visit of the British Fascist leader, Gerard Mandrake, in a few weeks' time. We both agreed that Goebbels has done a splendid job of propaganda in publicizing the meeting as one intended to promote peace and a lasting alliance between our two great nations and thus pave the way for a United Europe. The British newspapers have really gone to town on the affair, heralding it as "A New Era in European Solidarity."

The French press, I notice, are sour and generally suspicious, talking about the "Anglo-German Conspiracy" and forecasting a build-up in militarization. As if we gave a fig for their opinions. Their pathetic Maginot Line has made them the laughing-stock of Europe, and the Channel won't present much of a hazard, given the domination of British naval power.

When I suggested to Elisabeth that we go out to dinner one evening she blushed and pressed her head into her shoulder in a manner I found wholly enchanting. These strutting Rhine Maidens bore me, I must confess, with their loud voices and red cheeks and heavy bosoms. Elisabeth is dark, petite, and soft-spoken. Dare I say it—almost Jewish in appearance.

"I would be very pleased and most honoured," she said, "but perhaps you should know that I already have a young man. SS Sturmbannführer Heinz Mueller, a member of Himmler's intelligence staff. It would not be . . . proper for me to deceive him, Herr Doktor."

"Herr Doktor?" I chided her gently. "Surely you know me a little more intimately than that. After all these months. You must call me Theo."

Elisabeth smiled shyly. "I hope I have not offended you . . . Theo. I am most grateful, indeed flattered, that you should invite me out. It is an honour."

"Nonsense. Just because I am of high rank. You are a very pretty young woman. Beautiful, I should say. And I am not offended, not in the least. But I do not take no for an answer that easily. If your young man, your Heinz, should be posted away from Berlin—beware!"

We laughed together at this, and I could see her narrow pointed pink tongue and her small white teeth inside her soft red mouth, and the desire and conviction grew together that I would have her.. An army officer, of course, would have blundered in with both jackboots and frightened the poor creature and alerted her young man. But there are ways and ways. More than several ways, as the English say, of skinning a cat.

I have a new concoction. Like many of my ideas it came to me in the middle of the night. I had woken with the need to relieve myself and on returning to bed had lit a cigarette, one of the special brand made to my personal requirements.

Suddenly, out of nowhere, there popped into my head an idea for vitamin tablets. He's been babbling on for days now about supplementing soldiers' diets and it occurred to me—why not make them into sweets? Or better still, chocolate! Vitamin chocolate in each soldier's pack, what could be simpler, or easier to take?

I haven't so far mentioned this to anyone, not even the Führer, because ideas have a habit in the Chancellery of walking off and ending up on someone else's desk. Goering's, for example, that fat slothful beast. The idea I had for curing vertigo in trainee pilots was one day Item 9 on the conference agenda—proposed, it said, by the Reich Marshal himself! I racked my brains trying to recall who I'd discussed the idea with, but to no avail. And then I had to watch in silence as the fat pig positively swelled up with pride as he put forward "his" idea and saw the raised eyebrows and approving nods.

So this time I will talk to Felix first and ask his advice. If he assures me that the idea is practicable (and I don't see why it shouldn't be) we can go ahead and produce a trial batch in the factory. Then will be the moment to announce it to the jabbering apes.

Had a quiet word with Goebbels during the afternoon. He was passing by my office—deliberately going out of his way it seemed to me—and stopped to inquire after the Führer's health. I assured him that he was well and in good spirits, whereupon Goebbels lowered his voice and asked had I noticed the slight trembling in the Führer's left hand. As a matter of fact I had, and told him so, remarking that in my professional opinion it was nothing serious, probably nervous strain due to overwork.

"We are in the Führer's hands," Goebbels said in his quiet, even tone, always the mark of an educated man. "And the Führer is in yours. Never forget that. I wish you to know that you have my fullest confidence."

"Thank you, Herr Reichsminister," I replied. "If I can perform my duties with the same zeal and expertise as your good self none of us need have any worries."

A brief bleak smile passed across his face, and not being a man ready with his smiles it was reward enough. We understand and respect each other; that is my abiding impression.

I congratulated him on the birth of a son—his third or fourth I think it is—and he said, "There are many ways of making Germany strong. Frau Goebbels and I believe we have a sacred duty to build for the future. Young German manhood—our finest investment." Then his lean sallow face took on a humorous aspect and he said in a teasing manner:

"I trust you are investing in the future, Morell, even though you are a bachelor."

I assured him in the same jocular fashion that I was doing my utmost to ensure the potency and longevity of the Reich in an unofficial capacity.

"You do not have a regular ladyfriend?"

"Not as such," I answered carefully. "I would rather spread my investment. There is a particular young lady, Eva—I do not think you know her, Herr Reichsminister, a mutual friend of Hoffman—"

Goebbels narrowed his eyes. "The photographer?" He has an astounding memory for faces and names, even those he has met once and only briefly.

"That is correct. She works as a photographic model for fashion plates and the like. She is a good friend and companion. I will introduce her to you, if that is permitted. She would be thrilled to meet you."

"It is always *my* pleasure to meet charming young ladies," said Goebbels.

While he was in this relaxed frame of mind I thought it a

suitable moment to ask his opinion of the imminent visit by the British Fascist leader. Did he share the Führer's hopes that the meeting would set the seal on our plans for the next three years?

Goebbels considered for a moment. He is never one to utter rash pronouncements, without due thought. "A great deal depends on the attitude of the British Press. If there is the merest hint of warmongering I think the meeting could prove detrimental to our purposes. Mandrake is a clever man but sometimes his cleverness oversteps the boundary of plain common sense. He is not a pragmatist; he wants results now, quickly, without the bother of discrete and calculated moves in the right direction. We must send him home with something to crow about—but it must be the right thing, eminently sensible and praiseworthy in the eyes of the British people."

"You have discussed this with the Führer?" I inquired.

"The Führer, I think, appreciates the need for caution; his excesses will be held in check. But yes, to answer your original question, I believe the meeting to be absolutely crucial. Which is why the Führer's health concerns me. Everything possible must be done to safeguard his stamina and performance. I think you understand me."

"I do indeed, Herr Reichsminister. May I repeat that you need have no qualms in that direction. The Führer will be well cared for in every conceivable respect."

This chat enlivened my spirits considerably. Within the Chancellery it is easy to become secretive to the point of paranoia, believing everyone to be plotting against you in one way or another. Now I feel that my work has not gone unappreciated: Goebbels has tremendous influence and to count him as an ally in the maelstrom of inter-departmental intrigues is reassuring to me privately and prestigious in the day-to-day politicking which is such a wearisome feature of public office.

It has also been useful, I will not deny, in encouraging me to experiment with other preparations. One I have in mind is a sulphonamide compound which was injected into rats to increase their resistance to influenza and was by all accounts a great success. It hasn't been tested on human beings yet, though I don't see why it shouldn't have a similar prophylactic effect. In any case I can begin with small amounts and, all being well, increase the dosage over a period.

One fly in the oitment (felicitous phrase, ha-ha) is the constant interference by von Hasselbach, who just because he has treated the Führer in the past thinks he has sole authority to decide what medication should be prescribed. I will not tolerate this busybodying, and already I have a little plan hatching to put von Hasselbach's nose out of joint. If he isn't careful he'll find himself as junior medical intern in one of the camps Himmler is constructing in the Eastern Province. If the truth be told he's afraid that he's lost the confidence of the Führer and is now trying to stir up trouble at the slightest opportunity. He said to me the other day: "How can you prescribe those devilish Antigas Pills for stomach cramp? Heaven knows what foul poisons they contain."

My answer was that they did the trick: the Führer reported an immediate improvement—in a matter of hours, I told him—and was able to perform his ablutions without discomfort. These old-fashioned practitioners are really laughable in the way they cling to so-called "simple and natural" methods of treatment. Give me chemicals any day. "What are drugs for," I asked him, "if not to be used to treat patients? Next you'll be telling me to bleed him with leeches."

At this his face turned purple and the veins in his neck swelled up. "The question is one of diagnosis," he blustered. "Stomach cramps could have any one of a dozen causes, some of them serious. How do we know that the condition isn't operable?"

There I had him. The Führer, as is well known, cannot stand the sight of blood; the mere thought of it makes him feel faint and sickly, and so I said, "Are you, my dear Hans, proposing that we butcher the Führer? Are you going to open him up and poke around inside? And are you going to be the one to tell him?"

His face had lost some of its colour and his eyes went very small in his head. The idea of broaching the subject of surgery to the Führer had a tranquillizing, one might almost say (hee-hee) paralysing, effect. Von Hasselbach licked his lips and then blathered on for a while about "symptoms" and "diagnoses" and the dangers of what he termed "untried remedies."

"Then by all means put your point of view forward," I encouraged him. "You have my permission. I'm sure the Führer will listen to what you have to say in his usual calm and receptive manner."

I was smiling as I said this, and judging from von Hasselbach's expression he gathered from my kindly suggestion the inference intended. There was nothing more to be said. But any more pigheaded meddling from that quarter and I shall spike his career once and for all. In the Eastern Province he can meddle to his heart's content.

Returning from luncheon I saw Elisabeth and her young man eating their sandwiches in the Tiergarten. He is tall and blond and, I suppose, handsome in a brutal sort of way. All shoulders, arse and boots. I have never understood the mesmerizing effect that uniforms have on women. She was looking at him like a helpless young fawn, obviously totally entranced by his blond hair and black uniform and large red ears. He holds a lowly position in Himmler's circle of depravity but no doubt his true Aryan characteristics will guarantee a swift rise through the ranks.

Of that we shall see.

Berlin, August 1938

Mandrake made a splendid first impression on the Proletariat.

He has a tall, thin figure, ramrod-straight. Striking in profile and a natural showman. On the way from the airport he rode through the streets in an open car, standing next to the Führer, the pair of them saluting the cheering crowds and whipping them into a frenzy of excitement. Girls ran alongside and threw garlands of flowers into the car: a great festive occasion and just the right image to convey to the press and film cameras.

I was following in a staff car with Goering, Bormann and a member of the Abwehr, our much vaunted and totally useless Intelligence Service run by that dolt Canaris. Goering commented that the Führer seemed to have gained several inches in height, for he was on a par with Mandrake and yet on level ground shorter by a head. I saw Bormann and the Abwehr man exchange glances, though nothing was said. The fact of the matter is that I personally had anticipated what the drive might entail, i.e. the saluting, cheering crowds and so on, and had spoken to Erich Kempka, the Führer's chauffeur, and suggested that a small wooden platform be discreetly fitted into the car to make it appear that the two men were of equal height. This was done, thus saving the Führer from losing face (and height), and had been the cause of Goering's uncharitable and typically boorish observation.

Thank goodness we rarely see the man; yet even once a month in conference is once too often, and his disruptive and negative influence even then is disastrous to many a carefully-laid scheme. "The Father of the Luftwaffe" indeed—it's a wonder we have an air force at all with that cretin in command.

Mandrake spoke from the balcony of the Chancellery—in faultless German I am pleased to record—and it was quite apparent that the crowd had taken him to their hearts. Then the Führer stepped up to the microphone and delivered a magnificent speech, in full hot-blooded fervour, emphasizing once again the close links between our two great nations and calling on the rest of Europe to pay heed to "these two cousins," as he referred to them, joining together in selfless interest to promote the "New United Europe." "Let us be strong," he concluded, "because only in strength can we be magnanimous!"

This brought such a roar from the crowd that the Führer smiled and beckoned to Mandrake, who stepped up to the microphone and the two leaders linked arms in a stirring symbolic gesture which will surely go down in history as one of the most emotional and heart-warming embraces of all time. The noise was stupendous. I confess that my eyes were blurred at that moment, but blinking away the tears I caught sight of Goebbels, smiling and nodding enthusiastically, his narrow lean face aglow with the impassioned ferment of the crowd, the speeches, the spectacle. It was superlative stage-management.

Afterwards a reception was held in Mandrake's honour and I was introduced to him. He is a charming man, incisive, witty, and one of the shrewdest political analysts I have ever known. He gave his opinions frankly, yet at the same time was sympathetic to our difficult position *vis-à-vis* the Polish question. Interestingly enough he found parallels in Great Britain's attitude towards France, saying that the harassment of British shipping by the French Navy was something that, were he Prime Minister, would not be tolerated. This I took to be a reference to the recent incident in the English Channel when French gunboats intercepted a British cargo vessel and escorted her into Le Havre on the pretext that she was running contraband into the Channel ports.

A trumped-up charge, Mandrake maintained, and yet so far the British Government had hesitated to make any positive move apart from a tentative protest through diplomatic channels.

"It's a question of honour, is it not?" I said, and Mandrake readily agreed. I then asked what was the reaction of the British people to Press reports that the Reich was gearing itself for war. Did they accept such reports as being objective statements of fact?

Mandrake thought not. He said that the Press was sharply divided. Some newspapers and journals, notably those with a left-wing bias, were making all kinds of ridiculous claims about the so-called "German militarization programme" while other sections, the more sober-minded and sensible, calmly pointed out that every sovereign nation had the right and the duty to protect itself from potential agression.

His final judgment, I surmised, was that the British people

wanted some form of tangible reassurance that Germany was a peace-loving nation whose leaders sought nothing more sinister than to join hands with their "island cousins."

Bormann, standing nearby, had listened to all this in silence, just occasionally raising his heavily-lidded eyes, his square stolid face betraying no emotion. Now he spoke up and said that in his opinion the British people were short of only one thing—leadership. The people would follow if others were willing to lead. There was to be an election in the autumn, was there not? What better opportunity to put the hypothesis to the test?

Whether he was testing Mandrake or merely voicing an opinion I do not know: Bormann is an odd fellow, taciturn, morose, a real cold fish, and like the rest of his fishy race possesses a mind which normal warm-blooded creatures find difficult to comprehend.

In any case Mandrake would not be drawn. He nodded once or twice, which might have indicated assent or perhaps the politeness of a guest hiding his yawning indifference before one of his host's bumptious buffoons. The upshot of this was to increase my respect for Mandrake and harden the distrust and suspicion I already felt for the secretive and molelike Bormann, second-in-command to Hess.

It is three a.m. and I have just this minute returned from the Führer's bedroom. He relies on me more and more.

After the reception the toadying von Hasselbach suggested he rest for an hour, not knowing that I had injected him twice that morning with 250 mg. of dextrose and concentrated hormones. Consequently the Führer was in peak condition (essential for such an important occasion) and still keyed up with nervous energy. He gave von Hasselbach one of those blank yet curiously hypnotic stares which chill the blood of most people, saying that he would rest when he felt like resting and not a moment sooner. Von Hasselbach seemed to shrink visibly in front of us all, a gathering of forty or more in the Führer's private apartments overlooking the Chancellery gardens.

Goering, Himmler, Ribbentrop and several of the others looked at von Hasselbach piteously and then turned away as if he were a leper; his days in the Sanctum are numbered, of that there's little doubt.

Mandrake retired early, exhausted after his flight and the day's hectic celebrations, leaving about a dozen senior members of the Chancellery and their personal attendants. We stood in a large informal group with the Führer as centrepiece, still elated with the day's events and what he regarded as his own personal triumph of political strategy: the appearance of two great leaders in agreement over Europe and in perfect harmony.

His spring, you might say, was being wound tighter and tighter. As he talked he got carried away with his own inner vision, which in turn fed his eloquence and he went on and on, swivelling on the heels of his boots, his fingers jabbing stiffly to make a point, his right fist jerking up and down to drive home the importance of what he was saying, and then the fleshy smack as the fist hit the palm of his hand, doing this again and again and again.

His colour was high; his blue-grey eyes had taken on that dulled vacant expression as when a person is not in full possession of his faculties but following blindly the tenuous line of some driving inner compulsion. It was all there in his head: the others, to judge from their faces, didn't doubt it for a second. Yes, the vision was there all right, locked inside that cranium, but only *he* could see it—*they* saw it through him—being enacted in front of them by this short stumpy man with the glossy slicked-down hair and abrupt black brushstroke of a moustache.

I remember glancing at my watch and seeing that he had been talking without pause or interruption for almost forty minutes. The rest of the party, I'm sure, hadn't noticed the passage of time; they were spellbound by the Führer's voice as it went on and on with that barking staccato stridency which over a period tended to numb the senses. I could see he wouldn't last much longer. I looked over my shoulder and caught the eye of Julius Schaub, the Führer's adjutant. He read my meaning and moved quietly to collect my bag from the window alcove, placing it on a chair within easy reach. I indicated the assembly and nodded towards the tall doors leading to the ante-room, holding up five fingers, a prearranged sign that in five minutes the Führer would collapse and he was to clear the room and lock all the doors.

I was thirty seconds out in my calculations. The Führer paused in mid-sentence, his colour changed, almost as swiftly as it takes to set down the fact, and he took two faltering steps backwards. It might have been deliberate on his part, the others weren't to know, and for ten seconds there was absolute silence as everyone watched his rigid figure, the right fist curled and poised to crack into the palm, a faint smear of saliva gleaming wetly at the corner of his mouth.

Goebbels looked at once in my direction, sensing that something was wrong, and I nodded to Julius and pointed at the door. The room was cleared in under a minute, the doors were locked, and Julius returned to help me. Together we laid the Führer down on one of the couches, loosened his clothing, and from my bag I took out the syringe I had prepared: a 500 mg. solution of picrotoxin and morphine sulphate, a powerful stimulant combined with a narcotic relaxant. It was rather a large dose, the biggest so far, but his resistance to drugs is increasing at an astonishing rate.

His breathing was hoarse and erratic and his left hand, the entire arm in fact, was shaking uncontrollably as in palsy. At that moment he was probably unaware of his surroundings, though his eyes were wide open, staring, the eyeballs protruding.

"We should get him to his bed," Julius said.

"Not yet. The injection must take effect first. He'll be all right in a minute or two."

"Is he in any danger?" Julius raised the Führer's head and slipped a cusion underneath.

I didn't answer right away; it never does any good to let the layman believe the answer is simple, or alternatively that the doctor hasn't a clue what is wrong with the patient. If I let him sweat for a while it would increase his respect and dependence on me. So I pursed my lips and clicked my tongue, the learned practitioner mulling over the forces at war within the human organism, the mysteries of life and death.

"Julius," I said at last, gravely. "I will speak to you frankly. I wouldn't take you into my confidence if I didn't believe you to have the well-being of the Führer closest to your heart."

"Yes?" He moistened his lips. "Yes? What is it?"

"The Führer has an incurable disease," I said sombrely. "I have not told him this and neither must you. It is a secret known to just two people in all the world. Do you understand?"

"Yes," he whispered. His face was grey.

"We can save him, you and I, we can keep him alive—providing he is given the correct drugs in precisely the right amounts at certain times each and every day. Without these drugs he will die. Now I repeat, the Führer does not himself know of his true condition. He thinks it is nothing more than nervous strain due to overwork. The secret is between the two of us, you and I. No one, absolutely no one, must ever know the truth."

"You have my word, you can trust me," he said, his voice shaking. "On the body of my mother. Oh my God!"

The awesomeness of the moment, and of the knowledge I had sacredly imparted to him, suddenly struck home. His face, even his lips, were the same drab shade.

I said, "The value of your service to the Reich will be increased a millionfold if you can carry this secret within your heart. The Führer and the Fatherland depend on you."

After this little stirring speech, which almost brought tears to his eyes, I asked to be left alone with the patient, saying that it was necessary for me to observe him undisturbed for at least half an hour.

"We must allay the fears of the others," I told him. "I rely on you to make the announcement that the Führer is under sedation. Tell them he is all right and there is no cause for alarm. Say that I will issue a medical statement later this evening."

Julius went to the door.

"And by the way. If von Hasselbach requests, or even demands, to be admitted you must adamantly refuse. We cannot risk any further upset to the Führer's constitution at this critical stage."

"Very well, Herr Doktor. I understand. No one will be allowed to enter without your express permission."

A useful man, Julius; so trusting and obedient, determined to do his duty.

On receiving the injection the patient's eyes had grown heavy and gradually closed, but now as I pinched the skin on the back of his hand they fluttered open again. His gaze was vacant, still a little dull, though the pupils were no longer dilated. His skin was suffused with blood as the combined narcotic stimulant worked their way through his system. His first response on gaining consciousness was to start weeping.

"There, there now," I soothed him. "Nobody's going to hurt you. Everything is all right. Just lie still."

"I thought I was dead," Adolf said in a tiny voice like a child's. "I didn't die, did I?"

"No, of course not, silly goose. You're alive, here with me." I stroked his hand.

His eyes came into focus and he looked at me properly. "You're not my mother. Where's my mother? She said I mustn't talk to strange men."

"Now now now," I chided him, "let's have no foolishness. This is Theo, your doctor. You're in the Chancellery, remember? Your name is Adolf Hitler. You're the Leader of the Third Reich, Architect of the New Order, Führer of the united German peoples."

"Am I?" he said, blinking at me stupidly.

"Of course you are. Now pull yourself together, Liebling,

we can't let your disciples see you in this state. Come along now."

He struggled to sit up, the black slick of hair falling across his forehead. His left hand, I noticed, had slowed to a hardly discernible tremor.

"How do you feel?"

"Everything went suddenly dark. There was a rushing noise in my head. I didn't make a fool of myself, did I? The others, they didn't see. . ."

"Julius got rid of them, they saw nothing. It's all right, Adolf, there's no need to worry. Take it easy."

"What would I do without you, Theo? You're such a comfort. I'm all alone, nobody understands the burdens I have to bear, the tremendous responsibility. They all think I do it without effort, as though it doesn't require the most tremendous sacrifice and self-discipline." His hand gripped my shoulder.

"Depend on me, mein Führer."

"My dear friend Theo." He was about to blub again.

"Don't cry, Lieblichkeit*, Theo is here to look after you."

I took his hand from my shoulder and clasped it in both of mine. We remained like this for a while, Hitler weeping softly, and at length I cradled him in my arms and rocked him to sleep. The stimulant had done its job of reviving his shattered metabolism and now the narcotic was lulling his senses into deep slumber. In this semi-waking, semi-dreaming state I had found him to be at his most receptive. In the past I had implanted the seeds of a number of ideas (the vitamin chocolate for one) which had borne fruit days, sometimes weeks, later. Now was the time.

"This has been a wonderful day, Adolf," I began, rocking him to and fro. "A great personal and political triumph. The world will have to listen; the combined might of Germany

*Sweetness.

and Great Britain is invincible. Every nation on earth shall bow before it and pay homage."

"Invincible," he murmured sleepily.

"You are a great man," I continued. "The greatest military strategist of all time. Nothing can stand in your way."

"Nothing. . ."

"But I am concerned for you, Adolf. Some of your personal staff, those in whom you place implicit trust, are suspect in their devious motivations and insatiable ambitions. Certain members of Himmler's staff, for instance. I do not accuse Heinrich himself but I fear he is being misled by certain officers in his command."

"Mmmmzzz," Hitler mumbled, snuggling closer.

"You know it is not in my nature to harbour a grudge, Adolf, and I am loath to name names. But one SS Sturmbannführer Mueller is highly suspect, I might almost say treasonable. Certainly undesirable in a position of such potential power."

Sooner or later this would become manifest in orders of the day: a direct command that Himmler would have no choice but to carry out forthwith.

He was now, or so I thought, fast asleep, but as I laid his head on the cushion he stirred and said drowsily, "Do not leave me, Theo. I am so alone in all the world. Nobody really cares for me. Nobody." There was a catch in his voice.

"What you need, little friend," I said softly, the idea popping into my head from out of nowhere, "is the tender loving sympathy of a woman. Someone to listen to your troubles and care for you as I am doing. Wouldn't you like that, eh, wouldn't you, Liebling?"

"That sounds very nice. My own sweet edelweiss to comfort me in the dark hours before dawn. Find me someone, Theo. Blonde. Blue eyes. Healthy. A quiet sensible girl. . ."

His voice drifted away.

"I will find you someone." I smiled. "I have someone in mind already. You will like her, mein Führer. My little piece of horse manure."

He slurped his chops and started to snore.

Berlin, September 1938

Felix has sent me a sample of the vitamin chocolate and a report which pronounces it a great success. He has tried it out on the female workforce and apart from giving one or two of them diarrhoea it seems to be most effective. He even makes the claim that it might possibly possess the qualities of an aphrodisiac. Several of the workers, he reports, have been constantly in heat. (Not those suffering from diarrhoea, I hope! Ha-ha!)

Paid my customary visit to see Eva and spent a pleasant evening listening to the gramophone. She is not yet too keen on my proposal and I went to considerable lengths to stress the benefits: money, travel, luxury accommodation, security, etc. However, when she wants to be, Eva can be a stubborn girl, practically pigheaded, and I had to resort to a little touch of emotional blackmail.

There are two main obstacles to her agreeing, as I see the situation. First, the foolish tart professes to be in love with me (which naturally I can use to my advantage) and secondly—perhaps the major stumbling-block—she despises and detests the man.

Now this could prove a real hazard to my plans. Nothing, I have found, is so intransigent as the body chemistry of the female. I explained to her that personal feelings didn't enter into it—this was merely "an arrangement" and that she should regard it as an unpleasant task that would bring great rewards.

"But how *long* will it go on?" she demanded, obviously distraught at the prospect of spending months or even longer in the intimate company of somebody she found odious. "If it was one night I could get drunk and last out somehow till the morning. But you're talking about a relationship, something that could drag on for years."

"Darling," I said, "hush. Listen quietly now."

She turned to look at me, her face wistful in the lamplight. She has this maidenly habit of lowering her eyes demurely and glancing up through her fair lashes; very fetching it is, altogether quite effective; I'm sure he would fall for it. And something else in her favour: she is not a perfect beauty. He wouldn't go for that. But her winsomeness, the common-or-garden prettiness of a healthy outdoor girl with roses in her cheeks and fine unobtrusive features—yes, these are the ideal attributes.

"Now listen," I said, stroking her bare shoulder, "hasn't it occurred to you that you and I will see much more of each other? Here in Berlin and in Obersalzberg during the summer? Where he goes I go—we will be together, the three of us. And when he isn't looking. . ."

"You don't love me, Theo," she said pettishly. "If you did you couldn't bear the thought of another man touching me. Especially him. After all you've said about his personal bodily habits and the disgusting things he does in the bathroom."

She wrinkled her nose and shuddered.

My hand moved down to her waist underneath the bedclothes. She shivered and goose-pimples appeared on the soft hanging flesh of her arm.

"Listen to me," I said. "Think of it as a chore, a task that has to be done. It needn't be every night. You could ration him to once a week. In any case he'd be away some of the time on those mad schemes of his. You know how he likes dashing about, keeping people on their toes, pretending to be busy."

"Then you'd be away too," she pouted, arching her back in response to my silky explorations.

I held her nipple between finger and thumb and pinched it. It stiffened instantly. "Eva . . ." I crooned softly. "I'm asking you very nicely."

"Oh Theo, no, not even for you." She pushed my hand away. "You say you love me but you don't. You *don't*."

"Of course I do, my little horse-radish. Do this for Theo. It will make us very rich."

"Filthy rich?" she said, giving me the sidelong glance that

someone, possibly her first boyfriend, had told her was provocative. On a good day I'd give it six out of ten.

"Richer than all our dreams," I said, taking hold of her hands. "Ten times richer. A hundred times richer."

She pulled her hand from mine and brought it to rest on me beneath the bedclothes. Her eyes grew round. "One condition," she said, sounding out of breath. "That I can have this whenever I want it."

"Whenever he isn't looking," I qualified.

"You are a wicked, wicked man."

"Which is why you love me."

I clasped her buttocks and pulled her towards me; then disengaging one hand I took a piece of confectionery from the bedside table.

"A little present for you, dear heart."

"Oh Theo," she squealed. "Chocolate. How sweet of you." I popped the chocolate into her mouth. "You do think of me after all."

"That's my trouble," I sighed. "I'm just a foolish old sentimentalist at heart."

The news from abroad couldn't be better. On his return to England Mandrake was given the kind of reception usually reserved for conquering war heroes. With only two exceptions the British Press were ecstatic about his triumphant visit and the cordial welcome of the Chancellor and the entire German nation. There has been a good deal of speculation about the election to be held in October and how this new peace initiative will affect Mandrake's chances of becoming the next Prime Minister.

Today we received the newsreels, flown over by special courier, and Goebbels arranged a private showing during the afternoon. I thought this an opportune moment to introduce Eva to the Führer and telephoned the apartment, asking her to be at the Chancellery by two o'clock.

All went according to plan. We assembled in the conference room where the long table had been moved aside and the gilt chairs set in rows facing the screen. I was pleased to see that Eva had chosen a simple outfit for this important first meeting: a plain white blouse decorated with a subtle motif of alpine flowers (the Führer's favourite), a straight dark-green skirt and black low-heeled shoes. I had calculated that in flat shoes she would be smaller than him by five centimetres, which was absolutely crucial if the occasion was to be a success, and I was pleased to see that this was indeed so: the Führer "towered" over her, as much as he is able to tower over anyone.

After we had assembled I led her forward, having told her to keep her eyes downcast in a shy, diffident manner.

"May I crave your indulgence, mein Führer, in presenting to you Miss Eva Braun, who has implored me so many times to be allowed the privilege and honour of meeting you."

The first impression, I knew at once, was favourable, and several minutes passed in agreeable chatter. The Führer complimented Eva on her appearance and she responded with a small curtsy and a maidenly blush. The Führer smiled at this, glancing about him with eyes twinkling, and made what I think was a joke. Everyone laughed merrily.

When we sat down Eva was behind and slightly to one side of the Führer so that when he turned his head she was tantalizingly there at the corner of his vision. A quiet word with Julius had procured this happy arrangement.

The lights were dimmed and the screen flickered with numbers. The soundtrack crackled and then we saw a twin-engined aircraft coming in to land against a typically English sky of dark rainclouds. Mandrake stepped out and was immediately engulfed by an excited crowd. He was smiling in that rather tight-lipped way of his as he was led forward to a small platform and a cluster of microphones, surrounded on all sides by reporters and photographers. It seemed that the British Press regarded this as a major news story.

Goebbels had in his usual thorough way provided a transcript of the commentary and Mandrake's speech and I saw the Führer holding his copy to catch the light (he pretends that his English is good but actually he knows only a dozen words).

The camera had been moved nearer so that we had a large close-up of Mandrake, the wind ruffling his neat black cap of hair and the piece of paper he held in his hand. He smiled and nodded and started to speak:

"This morning I had a further meeting with the German Führer and we are agreed in recognizing that the question of Anglo-German relations is of the first importance for the two countries and for Europe. We both regard our meeting as symbolic of the desire of our two peoples never to go to war with one another again.

"We are resolved that the method of consultation shall be the method adopted to deal with any other questions that may concern our two countries, and we are determined to continue our efforts to remove possible sources of difference and thus to contribute to assure the peace of Europe.

"My very good friends, this is the second time in our history that there has come back from Germany 'peace with honour'. I believe it is peace for our time. I thank you from the bottom of my heart. And now I recommend you to go home and sleep quietly in your beds."

There was a great shout of laughter at this closing remark and even Goebbels was laughing aloud, a rare event. The lights went up and all eyes turned to the Führer, who was nodding enthusiastically and with a broad grin on his face. I saw him glance for just a second at Eva who was sitting primly with her hands folded in her lap. She was obeying my instructions to the letter, remaining quiet and unobtrusive, seemingly in awe of the company and the occasion. The first phase had gone without a hitch, as was confirmed to me later when Heinz Linge, his personal manservant, remarked in a quiet aside that "the Führer finds Miss Braun quite charming. He would not be averse to seeing her at the Chancellery in the near future."

"I'm sure Miss Braun would be delighted to attend," I answered.

Eva was standing by one of the tall ornate windows overlooking the Wilhelmstrasse and I strolled across and touched her lightly on the shoulder. She turned, the cold clear light emphasizing the slant of her high cheekbones. For some reason I remembered the mole on the inner curve of her right breast.

I said, "You were tremendous. He is very taken with you."

She looked at me and forced herself to smile; her eyes remained drab and without emotion. "Give me one of your cigarettes, those with the funny taste."

"My own special brand," I said, lighting it for her.

She coughed and said, "What a pathetic trumped-up little fart he is. I can't stand people with no sense of humour."

"He has a sense of humour. The trouble is that he laughs at all the wrong things. And the man himself is humourless."

"Yes, I suppose he must have a sense of humour," Eva said, holding the fixed smile like a mask, "otherwise with a face like that why bother to get up in the morning?" She looked into the room. "Do I really have to sleep with that bow-legged short-arsed toad?"

"Careful. Some of them can lip-read. I shouldn't worry too much about the sex thing. I'd be surprised if he could get it halfway up."

"What are you giving him at the moment?"

I caught Bormann's eye and nodded to him pleasantly. "Do you mean medication? Too many different things to remember offhand. I should say somewhere in the region of thirty different preparations. I might try something new on him in the morning, I haven't decided."

"Add bromide to the list, for Christ's sake," Eva said, smiling up at me with empty eyes.

The factory in Budapest is now in full swing and Felix is putting a new "line" into production: a sulphonamide we have called *Ultraseptyl,* which should be on sale to the public by Christmas. This is a compound I came across by accident when I was messing about in the Clinic one day. Felix says it tastes revolting, but people don't believe medicines are doing them any good unless they taste nasty; the nastier the better, I say.

The last three or four months have been extremely satisfying and fruitful—not to say lucrative. As concessionnaires for the combined armed forces we have our fingers, Felix and I, in many pies. And certain schemes which I instigated are coming along nicely, with just the odd nudge to keep them on course. Altogether a gratifying state of affairs.

Yesterday afternoon I came across Elisabeth crying in one of the offices upstairs. It seems that her young man (I vaguely recall he was on Himmler's staff) has been given a posting, without any warning whatsoever to the Eastern Province. I commiserated with her and suggested that dinner in a quiet restaurant I knew in the Unter Den Linden might help to take her mind off this painful separation.

She was reluctant until I happened to mention that I was on good terms with Reichsführer Himmler and that he might be persuaded to countermand the order. "There can be no harm in trying," I said, patting her shoulder. "After all, he's only human."

Elisabeth thanked me for my kindness and agreed to accept my invitation. We dined by candlelight at the *Biarritz* and she, in her misery I expect, drank more wine than was good for her. In any event I had to support her as we left the restaurant and she fell asleep on my shoulder in the cab. I rummaged in her bag and found the key to the front door and had to carry her upstairs to the first floor apartment.

Once inside I dumped her on the bed and went into the tiny kitchen to make black coffee. I do not like women passing out on me: it is rather futile, I always think, and such a waste when a woman cannot accommodate her partner's desires in the conscious state; besides which it is insulting to the partner to be faced with dry orifices in a comatose body.

Carrying her up the stairs had set the ache off in my shoulder, memento of a skiing accident in my youth when I had fallen heavily and lacerated the flesh. I swung my left arm a couple of times to ease the pain.

Elisabeth was still insensible. I made her swallow three tablets and wash them down with coffee. They stimulated her nervous system and she came groggily to her senses by which time I had undressed her and was preparing to mount. When she had recovered sufficiently to realize my intention she struck out with her fists and struggled to extricate herself from beneath my squatting embrace (I was astride her abdomen).

"Elisabeth," I said, catching hold of her wrists and pressing her arms to the eiderdown—she hadn't shaved her armpits, I noticed: "there's no need for all this. It's only me, Theo. You remember, Theodor Morell. I promised to speak to Himmler on your behalf."

She calmed down and lay there staring at me. Her eyes tense, frightened, though there was also a look—of sacrifice?—of resignation?—I did not recognize.

"That's better," I said, smiling down on her. "You won't help your young man by struggling, will you, Liebchen?"

She lay still, her breasts rising and falling, watching me, saying nothing, the rush of air audible in her nostrils.

"Open your legs for the doctor, there's a good girl."

She did so and it gave me pleasure to see her eyes contract and the spasm of pain cross her face as I entered her. She was tight and smooth, perhaps not quite slippery enough.

Pumping away, my face next to hers, I could see from the corner of my eye the dark straggle of hair underneath her arm and it suddenly occurred to me (all my best ideas come thus, instantaneously, out of nowhere) that if I could manufacture lice powder in bulk and supply the entire German Army my fortune would be made.

4

Proemptosis

"You blundered in where angels fear to tread," Johann Karve said, puffing pipesmoke into the air. It rose above his head like a grey wraith.

"You should have warned me that the woman was a hardliner." Queghan shook his head slowly, baffled, slightly irritable. "Why do people like that choose to work at MyTT? If they don't understand and sympathize with our aims why come here in the first place?"

"Professor deGrenier is an extremely capable scientist."

"I don't doubt it."

"And we do need such people. It's all very well when you go off on one of your blue sky sessions, or whatever you get up to in that monk's cell of yours, but without people like deGrenier the hardware to put your schemes into operation would never get developed." He regarded Queghan sternly from beneath his shaggy eyebrows.

"RECONPAN has nothing whatsoever to do with me. It was a Research Committee decision to fund it. I'm not responsible."

"No, that's right, I am."

"I'm sorry, Johann." Queghan got up and paced about. "It's just that the bloody woman wouldn't even meet me halfway. *I* don't know what's going on, I just have this instinctive feeling that something somewhere is wrong. But how do you explain that to a hardliner? DeGrenier won't accept anything unless it's in black and white on a cyberthetic print-out."

His annoyance, Karve realized, had deeper roots than Queghan was prepared to admit. Perhaps he felt guilty. The Director said casually:

"I don't suppose you looked into her mind."

Queghan carried on pacing. Finally he did say, "It wasn't intentional, maybe for a moment or two." He wouldn't meet Karve's eye. "She wouldn't realize, Johann. Probably feel uncomfortable and then forget all about it. It's second nature with me, you know that."

"Hardliners are suspicious of mythographers as it is without you poking around in their heads. And Pouline deGrenier isn't a fool, she'd guess what you were up to."

Queghan paced. He was tall and rangy but there was an abundance of nervous energy that his body couldn't contain. Karve knew that the physical activity was simply a displacement of intellectual frustration. Queghan was stuck for a direction and the signposts were either misleading or nonexistent.

"Did you read the CENTiNEL report?" asked the Director.

"Yes."

"Odd, isn't it?"

"I'd hardly describe the disintegration of spacetime as 'odd.' "

"You're being churlish again."

"It's the mood I'm in."

"Have we got it wrong, do you suppose? Is there another interpretation—a simple one—we've overlooked?"

"We're assuming the data are correct."

"They've been verified by cyberthetic analysis."

"As far as we know the rate of decay of mu-mesons has never altered. We know—we thought we knew—how they behaved, and now all at once we observe a series of particle interactions which don't fit the pattern." Queghan sat down. "Your guess is as good as mine."

"For heaven's sake, don't say that." Karve gave a wan smile. "My guesses aren't worth two a penny at present." He puffed some more smoke into the air. "If we go right back to the earliest phase, the time of the primeval atom, we know that there must have been an equivalent number of anti-protons and anti-neutrons in existence to complement the positively-charged particles—"

"Quantum theory tells us so but we don't know it for a fact. There was nobody around at the time to collect samples."

"We have to have a premise of some kind," Karve said, not unreasonably. "We didn't at one time believe in the existence of Temporal Flux Centres and now we find them throughout the universe. As the only man on the fourteen Colonized States to have been inside one I should have thought you'd grant me the courtesy of an accepted hypothesis."

Queghan said, "The thought in your mind is that I'm being churlish again."

"Yes."

"You're right, I am, carry on."

"So we have anti-particles. We also have White Holes, as complementary companions to Temporal Flux Centres; and we mustn't forget your particular favourites, the mythical anti-quark family."

"They'd never forgive you if you left them out."

"I wouldn't dream of it. Now as far as we know all anti-particles are existing in minus time, which is the mirror-image of the spatio-temporal frame of reference in which we and our universe exist. Am I going too fast for you?"

"I'm keeping up."

"Doesn't all this suggest something to you?"

"Not so far."

"I'll give you a word: proemptosis."

Karve sucked on his pipe and awaited Queghan's reaction. A long time, relatively speaking, elapsed. Then eventually:

"The mu-mesons are interacting with their anti-particle equivalents and therefore seem to be decaying before the appointed time. Hence proemptosis."

"Yes," Karve said, smiling faintly.

"In fact they might not be decaying at all in minus time.

We could be observing the process in reverse, like a film run backwards."

"The anti-matter universe interacting with our own. Exactly! Theoretically we know that it exists but we can never seem to point to a specific occurrence and say: 'There it is—the matter/anti-matter interface.' This might well be it, the specific point in spacetime where the two coexist."

"Is it testable? Could we devise a program for CENTiNEL to verify it?"

"I don't know," Karve said, shaking his head. "That's beyond the scope of Myth Technology. We'd have to talk to the astrophysicists. CENTiNEL is their baby."

Queghan mulled over the consequences of Karve's theory. And its pitfalls. How on earth could you devise a controlled experiment that had to take place in minus time? The very concept was, by definition, untenable. He tried to visualize this other universe moving on a reciprocal course in another stratum of spacetime: it would contain galaxies and nebulae, solar systems and planets, and presumably life of some sort. What was happening on these alternate planes of existence? What kind of history was being written on these anti-worlds existing in minus time? Perhaps a similar history to that of their own universe, yet with certain inconsistencies. . .

Supposing, Queghan thought, the idea suddenly taking hold, there was a person called Queghan (an anti-person) who was even now, at this moment (anti-moment), contemplating the possibility of another Queghan (himself) existing in an alternative universe? His alternate self, composed of anti-particles, sitting in an office on top of a pyramidal structure wondering if there was another version of himself?

An interesting cosmological and metaphysical speculation, Queghan (Mark I) thought wryly. And why stop at two? There might be fifty, a thousand, 10^{10} Queghans all busily contemplating their cosmic navels. But as usual he was running ahead of himself.

"Is it worth a try?" Karve asked.

"In the absence of anything else I'd have to say yes; but

how do we go about it? It's difficult enough trying to imagine a universe existing in minus time without having to conduct experiments there. But it can't simply be a mirror-image, can it? There must be other factors, other inconsistencies."

"That's where proemptosis fits in," Karve said, squinting through the pipesmoke. "The occurrence of an event before the calculated date. We have to sniff out any events which don't seem to follow in natural progression. It could be that their entire time sequence is out of kilter."

"Yes," Queghan agreed. "And maybe ours is too."

Queghan didn't swell on the mysterious Dr. Morell. Although it was still lodged in a corner of his mind and nagged at him now and then, the apparent "coincidence" was pushed aside and in its place he erected Karve's scaffolding of a hypothesis regarding the supposed matter/anti-matter interface. He pondered on this, and the paradoxical nature of minus time, the strange phenomenon of proemptosis, and all the while tried to discover a link, or "ley," which would connect one thing with another and so bring order to the random scatter of theory, instinct, blind chance and probability.

Another factor, which ought to have concerned him more, was his wife's increasing disorientation. She was inhabiting the real world less and less, concerning herself with detailed scenarios for historical reconstructions—at the moment researching mid-Twentieth America Pre-Colonization.

One evening after dinner he asked her why she was digging so far back into the history of Old Earth. "What is it that fascinates you?" Queghan asked, twirling the crystal brandy glass in his long fingers.

"That's where it all began. They must have had a special feeling for living, a reverence for natural things which we've lost."

"Not judging by the newstapes." Queghan too had studied the mid-Twentieth and made a number of mythological surveys. The era was rich in symbolism. "They revered the planet so much they almost killed it—the ruptured biosphere, remember."

"We *made* ours," Oria said. "We shaped it into a lump and hacked it around. The custom-built planet, suitable for all ages, races, colours and creeds." There was disgust in her voice.

"You want to return to nature?" Queghan mocked, "Become the protoplastic woman and start from scratch?"

"There's nothing wrong in trying to regain our roots."

"You sound like a sociology textbook. What roots? They're right here, all around you."

It was an argument they had rehearsed many times until it had grown stale. Queghan couldn't understand what drove her back into the past; it was an evasion of reality; neither could he understand why this should annoy him the way it did, and not understanding any of these things annoyed him even more.

Oria said, "You have your work. It fulfils you. You lose yourself in it and find yourself in it."

"You're a trained archivist," Queghan pointed out. He sensed chauvinistic blackmail and he wasn't having any. "If you want a job you could get one easily enough: MyTT would take you back tomorrow."

Oria covered her eyes. "Emotionally I'm blank. I can't feel for things. Everything tastes dead."

Queghan didn't know what to say to this. They went out into the garden. It was a calm night, the wind barely moving the leaves on the huge plane trees. The smaller of the two moons was a pale crescent rising in the eastern sky. The configurations of stars sharpened in icy brilliance as the darkness came on. Somewhere out there, Queghan reflected, shone the sun of Old Earth, too faint to be seen with the naked eye. An average star of no special significance, which somehow by accident had given birth to a species of intelligent creatures who so far were alone in the universe. It was true that their explorations had been tentative and minuscule in cosmic terms—no more than a few thousand light-years—and the galaxy must surely be teeming with life: the law of statistical probability made this fact self-evident. What would it do to the human race when the first shock of contact was made—the confrontation of alien cultures with nothing in common but the stars?

Some scientists believed that contact had been made already. Some of those engaged in MetaPsychical Research were of the opinion that intelligent life was at this moment communicating with the Colonized States but that human technology was incapable of deciphering the messages. They pointed to the radio chatter from the stars which, if only it could be interpreted correctly, would form a coherent signal from other beings elsewhere in the galaxy.

Queghan kept an open mind on this subject. The related sciences of Myth Technology and MetaPsychical Research sometimes worked at cross-purposes but in the long term they each contributed to the sum total of knowledge regarding man's place in the scheme of things. For instance, MetaPsychical Research had done much to relate human neurochemistry to the elemental forces of the universe, the "celestial clockwork of the Metagalaxy" as it was known to the purists.

In contrast his own field was concerned with psi phenomena and its relation to the four prime energy sources. They knew, and had known for a long time, that human thought could affect such random events as the radioactive fission of atomic nuclei. The production of "mind stuff" was a scientifically accepted fact, the research data were irrefutable; yet how and why this was so had still to be explained.

It was this search that had led him into the murky regions of quarks and anti-quarks, the genus of particles whose existence could not be proven but which had to exist if the material universe was an objective entity and not simply a figment of the imagination. "I think I am, therefore I am," was still the most telling proof of all for the ultimate reality of the mythical quark.

A bright steady speck of light came from behind the trees, heading due north. It was one of the satellite beacons circumnavigating Earth IVn: homing fixes for incoming shuttles.

Queghan felt a sudden yearning to go into space. It was like the call of the sea the old mariners had experienced, the compulsive biological urge to cross uncharted oceans and discover unknown continents. There was life out there somewhere amongst those billions of winking stars; they were calling to him, a vast cosmic whispering like the seductive lure of the sirens of ancient mythology.

The air had become slightly chill. The moon was now a brilliant slice of melon, perfectly clear and hard-edged against the night.

"Did you know it was the Americans who made the first atomic bomb?" Oria said. She was back in the mid-Twentieth, still seeking the roots of emotional response.

"So much for their reverence for natural living things."

"The first nuclear detonation took place on the 16th July, 1945 in New Mexico in the United States."

"I hope that isn't going to be the subject of your next historical reconstruction," Queghan said, and saw the gleam of a smile in the darkness. He still refused to believe there was anything seriously wrong with her.

Oria moved against him. How much was real and how much a jaded simulation? It was an uncharitable thought but one he couldn't dismiss. The accumulation of emotional debris that had built up over the aeons was like a log-jam in the mind; too many memories to accommodate within a single human brain. They were the most advanced of their species and had to carry the total collective consciousness of the race. It was a crushing burden.

"The Director wants me to talk to the CENTiNEL people. I shall have to visit the *Tempus* Control Laboratory."

"How long will you be away?"

"Not more than a week via the Field. Possibly two or three months on your time-scale."

"It isn't your job to go. Karve should send a physicist or go himself."

"He's an old man. A trip through the E.M.I. Field wouldn't do his cardiovascular system any good, even if they kept him in hyper-suspension. And in any case it is my job; the call of duty."

"What you mean is you're itching to go into space again, and you'll also be away from me for a while." But she said this with no rancour and it suddenly came to Queghan why, in spite of everything, they had stayed together all these years: he loved the woman, and if he had thought of looking into her mind he would have seen that she loved him.

The *Tempus* satellite Control Laboratory oribiting in the inertial frame of reference Theta^2 Orionis in M.42 was the deepest thrust into the void, a lonely outpost on the furthermost edge of manned exploration. It was uncomfortably, almost dangerously close to the Temporal Flux Centre x-ray designation *2U0525-06*.

From a distance the satellite appeared as a glittering six-pointed star, each of the arms a thousand metres in length, accommodating experimental laboratories, stimulose vegetable gardens, living space and recreational areas. Whenever he saw it poised against the star-filled backdrop Queghan felt the hairs rise on his spine that a man-made artefact could possess such awesome beauty. He became very aware of fragile mankind out here in dimensionless space, a soft-bodied bipedal primate gazing out at the universe like a child from its crib.

The transit shuttle docked and Queghan was greeted by the satellite Commander, Aldrin Laurence, a man with a large frame and a full dark beard streaked with grey. He ran *Tempus* as the old sea-masters had commanded the clippers, a mixture of rigid discipline tempered with paternal benevolence. It was a psychological tightrope he had to tread, a delicate balance to keep his crew and the scientific community in peaceable equilibrium. Out here there was nowhere to escape to; you had a job to do and it was the one hold on any sort of normality, the purpose that made life sane and bearable. And not far away—a few million miles—the unavoidable fact of all their lives: the inescapable presence of the Temporal Flux Centre, the datum point of infinite spacetime curvature where every law of physics was not only broken but twisted and distorted beyond comprehension.

During the first quarter-period Queghan stowed his belongings, took a nap, ate a light meal and acclimatized himself to the satellite's weak gravity. It usually upset his stomach so that while he continually felt the need to empty his bowels he was unable, when the time came, to perform the function. Karla Ritblat had prescribed some pills which helped to alleviate the predicament, but it remained rather distressing until his body had adjusted itself.

The CENTiNEL people were glad to see him. They were glad to see anybody. Johann Karve had outlined the purpose of Queghan's visit to the project leader, Professor Max Herff, and the first thing Herff said, even before Queghan had stepped through the door into the laboratory, was to express disappointment that a mythographer, "so accustomed to working in minus time, should feel it necessary to arrive before he departed."

"Rather mundane, I agree," Queghan replied. "But I thought that showing my arse before you saw my face might lead to some misinterpretation."

"How do you know we would have noticed?" said one of Herff's colleagues, a tall slender woman with a languid face and dark somnolent eyes; at no time during his stay did he ever see her upright—she was either leaning against something or lounging in a chair with her legs in the air.

Herff introduced him to the senior personnel and they quickly got down to the business of discussing the latest CENTiNEL report. Queghan had hoped for a clue that might shed some light on the recalcitrant mu-meson readings but the physicists were as baffled as he and Karve had been. Professor Herff, whose gentle manner, rumpled appearance and rimless spectacles reminded Queghan of a friendly family doctor, repeated that the figures made no apparent sense—"unless we're prepared to accept Karve's notion of the interactions taking place in minus time, wherever that is."

"If you have an alternative suggestion, Professor, I'd be happy to hear it." Queghan looked round at everyone. "Karve didn't propose his hypothesis for its novelty value; at least it's worth investigating."

"How do we go about it?" the tall languid woman, Dr. Zander, asked him. "Did Director Karve say how we should conduct the experiment? CENTiNEL is based in this spatio-temporal continuum, not in some mythical nether world. I should have thought astrophysics and not metaphysics was our line."

Herff said, "We're not going to start all that, are we? Queghan didn't make the trip from Earth IVn to engage in a debate on scientific demarcation."

"My apologies," Dr. Zander said, though she didn't sound apologetic or contrite.

Queghan pressed on. He wasn't going to get involved in that sterile argument. "Karve bases his theory on proemptosis. The idea is that the mu-mesons are being affected by time displacement so that there appears to be a discrepancy between the actual and the apparent rates of decay. On this side of the spatio-temporal interface we are observing the mirror-image of an event taking place on the other side."

"The other side being minus time," Max Herff said.

"That's right."

"Untouched by human hand," Dr. Zander said laconically.

Queghan chose to ignore this, though the sweat of mounting irritation prickled his shoulders and made the back of his neck damp. "Quantum theory tells us that when a particle and its anti-particle equivalent collide the result is instantaneous annihilation with a tremendous release of energy, mainly in the form of light."

One of the other scientists said, "That's the current theory behind the quasars, a super collision of matter and anti-matter releasing vast amounts of radiation."

"However, it's conceivable that under certain circumstances the particle and anti-particle can coexist—those circumstances being prevalent in the vicinity of a Temporal Flux Centre. If this is possible, and were to happen, a matter/anti-matter interface would be set up." He glanced round the circle of faces. "What I remember of quantum theory is rather sketchy, but one thing I've never forgotten is what would happen if we could isolate anti-particles and hold them for a controlled period in stasis—"

He became aware that Professor Herff was gazing at him with a peculiar expression on his face; it almost seemed as if he were about to break down and weep. Herff said:

"You do know what you're suggesting?"

"Yes," Queghan said soberly. "The ultimate energy source: the anti-matter bomb."

Dr. Zander laughed. It was a dead and humourless sound amongst the banks of instrumentation, the grey cyberthetic consoles, the ticking meters. "I see now why you're a mythographer. Anti-protons and anti-neurons held in stasis—impossible."

"I don't like to use that word if I can help it," Queghan said, conjuring up a pleasant smile for her benefit. She was an attractive woman but he felt like striking her.

"Now let's pursue this," Herff said, hunching forward, his hands clasped between his knees. "Anti-particles isolated for a controlled period: very well, quantum theory says it's feasible, so for the moment we'll accept that. But how do you account for the aggregation of anti-matter at a given spatio-temporal co-ordinate? That would seem to suggest a deliberate and systematic rationalization of energy and matter—that I find hard to take."

"I don't see why," Queghan said. "Somebody here has already mentioned quasars. We're not sure what they are but they're quite definitely the most concentrated source of energy in the observable universe. And we know they exist."

"Very well. As Riemann said, quasars could be the result of a collision between matter and anti-matter, we're not certain, but whatever causes them they do seem to be naturally-occurring phenomena, not planned or directed by. . ."

"An alien intelligence?" Queghan looked at Dr. Zander but she didn't rise to the bait. She was watching him closely and he couldn't read her expression. "Not once, in all these years of exploration, have we made contact with any other intelligent life-form. Naturally we're expecting them to be humanoid, to have two eyes, a nose, a mouth, and, if male, a five o'clock shadow. Isn't it more likely that they're in a form we don't recognize as life, crystalline perhaps, or gaseous, or even sub-nuclear? Mankind is a biological accident, a freak life-form that just happened to evolve on a cosy planet near a friendly sun. I'd find it much more credible, if I were writing the scenario, to make my life-forms more in keeping with the organic structure of the universe I was constructing—matter and energy in their constituent parts. And that applies equally to anti-matter existing in minus time. It's arrogant pigheaded chauvinism to believe otherwise."

"A self-aware intelligence composed of anti-matter," Herff said, tasting the sound of it.

"Not necessarily. The intelligence could be of our universe, using anti-matter as an energy source, either for constructive or destructive purposes."

"The anti-matter bomb," Dr. Zander said. She was vaguely amused. "The ultimate weapon."

As if suddenly waking up to the notion Herff said, "If there was an intelligent life-form composed of sub-atomic particles—mu-mesons, leptons, hadrons, whatever—it couldn't find a more efficient energy source than anti-matter, providing it could exercise proper control."

"Particles controlling other particles," Queghan said. "It doesn't sound so very different from people controlling other people."

Riemann said, "But for what purpose? Any of this might be feasible, it's more or less implied by accepted quantum theory, but that still leaves the question Why? What is it trying to achieve?"

"Do you suppose a protoplasm can comprehend our world?" Queghan said. "Does it even know that we exist? And supposing it did know, how could it communicate with us? We're in the position of a protoplasm in relation to a life-form composed of sub-nuclear particles. Perhaps it knows that we exist, just as we know the protoplasm exists, but its means of communication are beyond our senses and our technology. How do we *begin* to communicate with something that lives in space, that can travel between galaxies at lightspeed, whose time-scale is measured at one extreme in thousand billionths of a second and at the other in millennia, that can pass through solid matter as though it was a hazy patch of mist? How can we ask the purpose of a life-form so alien to our own that its presence is only apparent as a trace on a photographic plate? You might just as well ask that chair you're sitting on if it believes in the existence of God."

"Is this how mythographers spend their time?" Dr. Zander inquired dryly.

"Do you mean inventing fictions?"

"No, please don't misunderstand. I'm not trying to be clever at your expense."

"You're not?" It was Queghan's turn to be sardonic.

"I'm intrigued at the way the mind of a mythographer works. You seem to attack a problem in several different directions and on a number of levels simultaneously."

"I take that as a compliment."

"It wasn't meant as criticism."

"If you mean that mythographers can provide the questions but not the answers I'd have to agree; the only sense I trust is my instinct."

"So you've brought the questions along and it's up to us to find the answers?" Dr. Zander said, lounging in her chair.

"Not the best of bargains I agree," Queghan said. "I don't even know where to start looking. But at least you have the Particle Accelerator; one or two of the answers might be lurking there."

"If we knew what we were looking for."

Max Herff said, "I don't know if my instinct is in as good a working order as Queghan's, but I suggest we set up a program of anti-particle investigation. If we can locate an inverse shift in radioactive decay which corresponds to the mu-meson findings it would at least be an indication that we're heading in the right direction. Where we go after that I haven't a clue."

"What temperatures are you operating at?" Queghan asked.

"Ten billion degrees," said Riemann.

"Can you go higher?"

"We could," Riemann said cautiously. "It might create problems with the Dyson Electromagnetic Sphere. The Sphere is holding the Temporal Flux Centre in equilibrium by means of a one-million-volt field. A major increase in temperature could upset the balance." He looked uncertainly at Max Herff.

"How high do you want to go?" Herff said.

"One thousand billion degrees."

There was an absolute stunned silence. Riemann laughed nervously and it turned into a fit of choking. Dr. Zander said, "The impossible we can do right away. Miracles take a little longer."

"One *thousand* billion?" Herff said. He had the crinkled weeping look on his face again.

"That would seem to be the region if we're chasing the anti-matter equivalents to the mu-mesons," Queghan said. "At temperatures above one thousand billion degrees we get the entire range of hadronic particles and their anti-matter companions."

There was a further silence while everyone adjusted their mental horizons to the power of 10^{12}.

Finally Riemann ventured to say, We could do it by raising the energy component to correspond to that temperature. That's the only way I can see."

Dr. Zander smiled. It was a genuine smile, if rather bemused. "When you have a hunch," she said to Queghan, "you sure do have a hunch."

5

Shades of Deadly Night

Pouline deGrenier sat alone in the darkened office. Through the curved panel to her left she could see the flickering display of lights in the laboratory: symmetrical patterns of red, green, orange and magenta glowing momentarily in sequence and then going out, glowing, going out as in some mysterious and inexplicable ritual. Now and then came the faint whirr of a timing device followed by the subdued *click* of a circuit-breaker disconnecting itself according to predetermined plan.

There's something satisfying about machines (this was the thought preoccupying her); care for them and see to their needs and they won't let you down. It was a good feeling to know they were working selflessly, tirelessly, through the night, keeping temperature, pressure, saline content and the other vital processes within the safety parameters. Alert for the merest hint of trouble.

She wondered, in a detached sort of way, what need it was fulfilling—in her. Was it that she had control, that the machines were docile obedient slaves willing to do anything she asked? Did everything, in the end, come down to the ego's insatiable driving greed for self-assertion, for power, for the right to indulge itself at the expense of other people, other things, everything not of the ego itself?

I'm not an ambitious woman, she thought, I'm really not. I want the project to be a success, I want to see it work as it was meant to work, but I don't seek the power that Karla Ritblat has made the absolute reason for living. She craves it like a drug. Nothing must stand in her way, and if something does, it must be swept aside regardless of human feeling. But wasn't Karla Ritblat in the process destroying the point of her work, its essential purpose and meaning? Scientific achievement didn't operate in a vacuum, it wasn't an end in itself. Its purpose, surely, was to advance humanity, to provide knowledge that would ultimately be of benefit to mankind, to make human beings more aware of their humanness. Karla Ritblat, in losing sight of this, might just as well have been one of the machines in the Psycho-Med Faculty, as cold and bloodless and detached as an electroencephalogram.

Pouline deGrenier shuddered. I mustn't become like that. I'm alive, I want to live, I want to love a man and have babies. Without these things what is the point in being a woman?

She touched her breasts and felt the faint stirring of quickening response. Her body was seeping fluid and she was both excited and ashamed of herself. Is it possible . . . could I invent a machine to make love to me? she wondered, and at once smiled at the absurdity of the idea. It was also rather sad—she knew this too—that a healthy woman in the prime of nubility should entertain such thoughts.

"You're short of only one thing, Pouline deGrenier," she told herself aloud, with mock sternness, "and that's a good fucking."

The sound of her own voice startled her. She glanced round: was someone out there in the shadowed laboratory, listening to her? She almost made herself believe that there was—a man undoubtedly, a secret lover spying on her, watching her face and reading her thoughts.

She thought it so ironic that despite mankind's progress through the centuries, the advances that had been made in every branch of human endeavour, that despite all this the human race was still shackled to the basic biological urge: the genitalia were now, as ever, the focal point of existence, constant reminder that the species hadn't really progressed beyond its origins as a cave-dwelling tool-making primate at the mercy of its neurochemical instincts.

There was a sound from the laboratory—the *click* of a circuit-breaker—and Pouline roused herself from this mood of morbid introspection. She thought: I'm getting to be like an old maid. Next I'll be looking under the bed in case—let's face it, in the hope—there's a man hiding there.

She went through into the laboratory and stood for some minutes listening to the hushed electro-mechanical purr, the soft gurgling fluids and clicking relays, watching the dials in their green fluorescent portholes. It was beautiful, it was all very beautiful: she felt a nervous thrill in her stomach and upper arms—RECONPAN was her baby! A new and completely original technique to recreate in the thermoplastic the brain of someone long dead. There was no actual cranium of course (science still couldn't emulate nature to that degree of sophistication) but they had been able to achieve, using solid-state germanium micro-circuitry, a precise simulation of billions of neurological cells linked by electrochemical pathways.

Every component of the brain was faithfully reproduced in the units ranged against the walls; the cerebellum, the cerebrum, the cerebral cortex, the limbic system and the reticular activating system, and along the ceiling a gantry carried thick multicoloured cables representing the bundles of nerves—the corpus collosum—connecting the two hemispheres of the brain.

The major problem had been to artificially stimulate the tissue cultures to receive and transmit electrochemical data. Originally they had hoped to construct the brain entirely of germanium circuitry but tests had shown that what in fact they were creating was not a brain at all—something not dissimilar to the cyberthetic system. The tissue cultures, immersed in a solution of proteins, amino-acids and inorganic salts, were essential if RECONPAN was to possess the qualities which made the human brain a unique organism: self-awareness, memory, innovative feedback, and above all the capability to think, to reason, to make decisions.

This was where Karla Ritblat had become involved. As head of the Psycho-Med Faculty she was the Institute's specialist in organic structures. The problem, only recently overcome, was how to make the tissue cultures receptive to electrochemical impulses; without this facility the brain would have been able to store millions of memory traces but wouldn't have known what to do with them—rather like a gigantic data-handling complex where the janitor had forgotten to turn on the power. It was all there but it wouldn't work.

Now it should. The research involved had been painstaking and the technology highly advanced: each individual neuron cell in the human brain operates on a power requirement of one one thousand millionth of a watt; the entire brain needs only ten watts to function normally. The problem facing the RECONPAN team was how to power the multi-billion celled complex without overloading it and blowing every circuit. It would have been comparable to a person suffering a severe and permanent brainstorm—nothing remaining but a blank-eyed autistic zombie.

Standing before the winking patterns of light in the darkened laboratory, Pouline deGrenier hoped and prayed that it was a problem solved. They wouldn't know for certain until experimental trials began in twenty-four hours. She thought with a sudden spasm of fear: *Twenty-four hours*. Was it really so near? After all the grinding effort, the years of work, the meticulous research . . . she didn't want it to start. It was too final. The thought of failure numbed her. Better to travel in hopeful expectation than to arrive. But this, she knew full well, was foolish thinking.

You're behaving like a female, she admonished herself, and immediately thought, What the hell, that's what I am. Female. I should go out and celebrate. Have a drink, share a joke, have a laugh, get laid—

It kept coming back to that. The project she had worked so hard to complete was like the taste of ashes in her mouth. Perhaps I'm a biological freak, she thought giddily, and swept her arms open and addressed the question to the watchful waiting laboratory. Are my needs excessive, are they base and ignoble?

The cabinet in front of her clicked a non-committal reply and the pattern of lights changed sequence. She moved closer to the machine and pressed herself against its humming and vibrating body. The high-frequency oscillations jarred her pelvic bone and she pressed harder, holding the cabinet like an awkward lover, feeling its mechanical caress penetrate deep inside. She said, this time in a whisper, "Oh yes, I need you. I need somebody. Somebody please take me."

She thought crazily, If a man walked in now, this minute, he could have me. I would offer myself. Anybody, any man, no matter who it was, would do.

And again she said aloud, holding the machine tightly, "I want Queghan to walk in and take me. I'd say to him, 'Please take me. What I need is a damn good fuck and I want you to do it to me. Do it to me. Oh shit, do it, do it, please . . .' "

She tasted salt on her lips and realized that she was crying. She was wet elsewhere.

Well now. Professor deGrenier. This is not the kind of behaviour becoming to a scientist and a lady. And then she thought, This silly stupid female business acting up again. Why do women have to cry? What do men do in place of crying? Are they as tough and hard and controlled as they seem or is it all show, mere masculine display? In place of crying they must do something.

She looked at her watch. It was one-forty. Without another thought and with single-minded intent she returned to the office and pressed the code that would connect her directly with his private line.

When Queghan saw his wife again she scrutinized him closely and said: "How many this time?"

"Is it beginning to make a difference?"

"It's very upsetting for a woman to have a husband who

looks younger than she does," Oria said. "It sets people talking. Every time you come back from *Tempus* I expect to see you looking like Dorian Gray."

"Remember what happened to him."

"Well, how many?"

Queghan thought for a moment. "Ten."

"You're sure it's not more?"

"How long was I away?"

"Nearly three months."

"That's near enough then." Queghan counted on his fingers. "I spent one week on *Tempus,* which coincides roughly with Earth IVn time; add a week for travel through the Field. So I aged two weeks in real-time while three months passed by here. Two weeks from twelve is ten."

Oria still wasn't happy. "Don't you think it would be a good idea if wives were permitted to take a trip through the E.M.I. Field? That way we could keep up with our husbands. As it is, we're going in opposite directions—I'm heading for the grave while you're regressing to the cradle."

"I'm two years older than you to begin with," Queghan pointed out.

"You *were* two years older. According to my reckoning we're now about the same age, and it isn't doing my morale any good."

Queghan laughed. "You always make the mistake of assuming that I'm getting younger—I'm simply ageing more slowly than you are. Time dilation in the E.M.I. Field* doesn't reverse the ageing process, it slows it down by a variable factor depending on the velocity of the traveller relative to lightspeed."

"So when I'm sixty-five you'll be celebrating your fiftieth birthday. 'Who's that with you?' they'll ask you. 'Your mother?' "

"Don't worry about it. As an extra-special birthday treat I'll arrange a long trip for you—a month or so in the Field—

*For a technical explanation of the E.M.I. (Electromagnetic Interference) Field and the effects of time dilation, readers are referred to the first book in the "Q" Series: *Seeking the Mythical Future*.

and when you get back we'll be the same age. You might even be younger."

"But I'll be away all those years waiting for you to catch me up!" Oria wailed.

"No," Queghan said patiently. "You'll be away just one month on your time-scale. It's me that's going to have to wait for you. A month in the field is . . ." he did a quick rough calculation ". . . approximately nine years. But to achieve that you'll have to spend a month in hyper-suspension at a fraction below lightspeed."

Oria meditated on this. She said suspiciously, "Does that mean you're going to be left on your own for *nine years* while I'm shuttling about in spacetime somewhere?"

" 'Fraid so," Queghan said, poker-faced. "There isn't any other way it can be done."

Oria went and looked at herself in the mirror. "That's a tough decision. To lose nine years in age or to have my husband running around loose for all that time. I can't win either way," she told her reflection. "If I don't take the trip some young bright-eyed girl will come along and snatch him away from the aged hag he's living with, and if I do go into the Field he'll be fancy-free for nine years."

"Would you like to be left alone while you decide?" Queghan inquired solicitously.

"You might think it funny," Oria said, turning from the mirror.

"I'm not laughing."

"What's that expression on your face?"

Queghan beckoned and she came to him. "What have you been doing while I've been away?"

"Getting steadily older."

"If you go on like this it'll become an obsession."

"It is an obsession. If you must know I've hardly been out of the house. Run off my feet most of the time. Slaving over a hot stove. Hardly a minute to call my own."

"I thought we'd moved on from the D. H. Lawrence phase?"

"We have. I'm into mid-Twentieth America now."

"You'll have to change your vocabulary. Americans in the mid-Twentieth didn't, I'm quite sure, use the phrase 'Slaving over a hot stove.' "

"What phrases would they have used? I haven't got round to researching the semantics of the period. Would they have said 'Run off my feet?' "

"It doesn't sound right somehow. Their talk was much more clipped, epigrammatic. Remember the film we viewed in Archives? What was that line—'I'll love you, baby, till hell freezes over.' "

Oria said, "I can't go round saying that. Who would I say it to? Are there no other lines you remember?"

"Mm," Queghan said after a moment. "How about this: 'Here's looking at you, kid?' "

" 'Here's looking at your kid?' " Oria repeated, staring at him. "What does it mean?"

"I was trying to do the accent. The line is: 'Here's looking at *you,* kid.' "

Oria said this several times but still didn't understand it. "I like the sound of it but what does it mean?"

"It means . . . well I suppose it means . . ." Queghan rubbed his nose. "Does it really matter? If it sounds all right why not use it?"

Oria looked doubtful. "I'd better check on it first; I want to use it in context."

"How's the rest of the research coming along?"

"I used the cyberthetic system at MyTT while you were away. It saves a lot of time—it gave me a complete dossier on the life profile: fashion, furniture, transportation, social mores—"

"But not speech patterns."

"I never asked about that."

"You should study the newstapes in Archives," Queghan recommended. "You'll be able to see how the people actually looked and behaved and spoke. Have you chosen a decade?"

"The 'Fifties. It was just after their Second World War and everything was changing rapidly. It's an interesting period."

"Which is how you came to know about the first atomic bomb," Queghan said.

Oria seemed suddenly preoccupied. She had drifted away, as she did on occasion without warning. "Yes, that's right," she said, her face clouded.

"Are you all right?"

"Yes," she said, nodding, and then: "There was something in the dossier that didn't make sense. At least I couldn't understand it."

"What was it?"

"I asked the cyberthetic system for items of interior decoration to make the reconstruction authentic. Amongst them was a list of popular household plants: daffodils, roses, tulips, something called chrysanthemums, rubber plants, and so on, and right at the end, deadly black nightshade."

Queghan didn't say anything. He was breathing lightly and evenly.

"I couldn't understand it so I looked up the classification in the encyclopaedia. The botanical description of a night-is *Solanum nigrum*. It's also known as morel." Oria sighed. "It didn't make sense even then."

"I don't suppose it would."

He had waited patiently and was now rewarded. There it was, large as life: the third coincidence.

Queghan reported to the Director on his visit to the *Tempus* Control Laboratory. Karve was amused at Max Herff's reaction to the proposal that the search for the elusive anti-particles should take place at an average mean temperature of one thousand billion degrees. He bit on the stem of his pipe, shaking his head and chuckling to himself.

"He really looked as if he was about to cry," said Queghan, standing at the angled window on Level 40. The campus below looked fresh and green in the clear morning light.

"What do you estimate their chances to be?"

"I wouldn't have said high."

"Neither would I. But I have every confidence in Max; he might not welcome you with open arms the next time you meet but he'll do his best with CENTiNEL."

Queghan looked at the Director. "Let's be honest, Johann, we're dealing with a range of sub-atomic particles we know very little about, and when we start talking about anti-matter and minus time we're like infants trying to grapple with Einstein's Unified Field equations." It struck him, and not for the first time, that Karve was not too dissimilar in appearance to Einstein: the same flowing grey hair, broad Semitic nose and deep-sunk eyes—he even smoked a long-stemmed pipe as the father of Pre-Colonization physics had done—though Karve lacked a straggling moustache to complete the image. "If you want an opinion I'd say that the law of probability will have a lot to do with their chances of success. They might find the anti-particle equivalents in six months, ten years, or it could be tomorrow—"

"And then we face the real question: what do we do with the data once we have it."

"That's what none of the CENTiNEL team bothered to ask," Queghan said. "They were interested, it was obviously a challenge, I could see it in their eyes, but what happens if we find that a genus of sub-atomic particles is meddling with spacetime and affecting organic structure? We can't understand them, we can't communicate with them, we don't know what their purpose is. They're probably totally oblivious to our presence. So far as they're concerned we could be a bizarre and not particularly interesting astrobiological specimen, a smear culture on a laboratory slide that's hardly worth a passing glance. What they choose to do with the fabric of spacetime and the structure of matter is in their own interest and doesn't concern us; we happen to be in the position of an unfortunate bystander caught up in the process. Tough shit for the human race."

After a moment's rumination Karve said, "But it doesn't follow that we're powerless. We have CENTiNEL and we also have control, to a limited degree, of a Temporal Flux

Centre. These are not inconsiderable technological achievements."

"I suppose you're right," Queghan said, not convinced.

"And we also have your gift for mythic projection."

"Is that significant?"

"Don't you think so?"

"I don't know." Queghan came away from the window and sat down in the ergonomic chair. "How exactly?"

"If our assumptions are correct and the anti-particles are in fact disrupting spacetime, what are the ways in which this will become apparent to us? They won't only affect time present, the here and now, but also the past and the future."

"They could affect the past?"

"Most certainly. The law of causality isn't sacrosanct. Do you suppose anti-matter is any respecter of our neat and tidy earth-bound rules? If it affects time it will affect all time, and with it causality. Cause and effect is a direct corollary of spacetime. Therefore if spacetime *is* being disrupted it follows that cause and effect will get a pretty rough ride too. There will be . . . inconsistencies."

Queghan mulled this over. He envied Karve's powers of didactic reasoning. He said eventually, "So somewhere in the past we should come across events—happenings?—which have been altered in some way. They will go against recorded history as we know it."

"To be honest I don't really know, Chris. I'm simply taking the data as supplied by CENTiNEL and interpolating a series of possible consequences."

He looked at Queghan for a long moment and then from a drawer took a file sheathed in green vinyl. He said casually:

"Did you know that the Germans were the first to develop the atomic bomb? They made and tested a prototype by the autumn of 1943 Pre-Colonization."

Queghan was surprised and intrigued. "No, I never knew that."

"Neither did I," Karve said, smiling. He extracted the file from its sheath and opened it. "How's this for an interesting and little-known fact: the British Blackshirts were voted into office on the 30th October, 1938, with Gerard Mandrake as Prime Minister."

"Do you mean the Fascist party?"

Karve nodded and turned a page. "Surprising how ignorant we are of Pre-Colonization history," he remarked lightly. "How about this: Germany invaded Poland on the 9th May, 1939, and three days later Great Britain launched a sea- and airborne invasion of France which met with only token resistance. Within three weeks, by the 3rd June, France and her dependencies were occupied territory under the sovereign rule of Great Britain. The French Government capitulated and all power was vested in the Acting Consular-General, Sir Richard Brock-Tregenna."

"What is this, the synopsis for a novel?"

"The Anglo-German Peace Pact," Karve went blithely on, "was signed in the autumn of 1939, on the 3rd September, and one month later, to the day, a combined force of British and German troops crossed the border at Zbereze, and Russia, having entered into a treaty to protect the Ukraine, declared war. By Christmas the two sides were engaged in full-scale battles along nine hundred miles of frontier—"

"Before you go any further with your fairytale would you mind telling me what it's supposed to be?"

The Director held up the file so that Queghan could see the word RECONPAN on the cover. "These are the pronouncements of one Adolf Hitler," Karve said. "Or perhaps it would be more accurate to say the simulated brain of Adolf Hitler." He laid the folder on the desk. "You look perplexed, Chris."

"Bloody mystified. What information have they fed into RECONPAN to get stuff like that?"

"Nothing wrong with the research, not a thing. They utilized every scrap of information in Archives and it's all been cyberthetically processed and verified. I can't fault their industry, nor their scrupulousness." He glanced down at the folder. "As far as we can tell this is a true and factual account."

"A true and factual account of what?"

"Of what took place."

"But it didn't take place. I'm no historian but I know the outlines of Pre-Colonization history on Old Earth. This is a complete distortion of what actually happened."

Karve's pipe had gone out and he took a moment or two to relight it. When it was going merrily again he said, "We were discussing a possible breach in causality a while back. Certain 'inconsistencies' were mentioned; do you suppose these are they?"

Queghan flexed his long fingers and pulled at the lobe of his ear. "Disruption of the mechanics of cause and effect," he said abstractedly.

"It wouldn't require a major shift of emphasis; a minor detail in historical terms; merely a footnote so to speak. The actions of one man, say, influencing those of another. From a single insignificant alteration could spring a chain of events which would culminate in a complete reversal of documented historical evidence. History turned upside down."

"In mythological terms there's no reason why that shouldn't happen," Queghan said. "But we already have documentation which states that certain events took place at certain times. How does that square with the RECONPAN findings? The two are directly conflicting."

"Not necessarily—and only if we make the mistake of trying to cram both sets of events into the same spatio-temporal datum point. Both could quite conceivably have taken place, separated in time and space by . . . I don't know." He waved his hand. "Something or other."

"The matter/anti-matter interface."

They looked at each other.

Queghan indicated the folder. "These events took place in a world composed of anti-matter. Isn't it possible? And of course we wouldn't have any record of them because they happened on the other side of the interface."

"In minus time."

"*Yes,*" Queghan said, his face transformed. Suddenly he smiled and laughed out loud. "Didn't you once tell me that

RECONPAN was pure research? It looks as if it's an indispensable technique for investigating alternative mythologies. I think we shall have to be rather more considerate to our good friend and colleague Professor deGrenier."

"I wasn't aware that *I* had been inconsiderate," Karve said dryly. "As I recall—"

"Yes, well, of course." Queghan rubbed his chin and stared over the Director's head. "I suppose I'd better do something about that."

"I suppose you had."

"I shall proceed with all due caution." It occurred to him to ask: "What does deGrenier make of this? Did she think the cerebellum had blown a gasket?"

"She passed it along without comment." Karve eased himself away from the desk and steered his chair to the window. He would have been a normal-sized man but for his legs. He said, "I don't know if this has crossed your mind but it strikes me as being rather odd: deGrenier fed the correct information into RECONPAN and yet it came up with the 'wrong' events. How do you explain that?"

"I don't know if I can."

"Doesn't it strike you that some kind of manipulation is taking place?" The Director swivelled his chair into the room. "Something inside that machine in the RECONPAN laboratory is recreating a new set of historical facts, an alternative scenario. Is it the brain itself or is it being affected by an external agency? If we knew the answer to that we might be a step nearer to understanding the mind of an intelligent life-form composed of anti-matter."

"Is it a mind we would understand?" Queghan wondered aloud. "Is it a mind at all in the sense of the term as we understand it?"

"If it possesses intelligence, then there has to be a way of establishing communication."

"How?"

"Through the RECONPAN facility, via the brain itself." Karve paused and looked at Queghan, his gaze steady and unblinking. "I said a moment ago that one of the advantages we have in this establishment is your talent for mythic projection. If you can work together with deGrenier, using the RECONPAN facility—''

''Hold it there. You want me to sit in the RECONPAN lab conversing with the brain of Adolf Hitler?''

''Not only conversing. You must try to project yourself into this mythical other world. We don't know what's going to happen there and neither do we know how this alternative scenario will work out in the end.''

''RECONPAN will provide that information.''

''That's true. What it won't do and can't do is influence events in any way. We are, to use your phrase, in the position of an unfortunate bystander—unless somehow we can intervene and shape those events, alter their direction.''

Queghan went to the window. The world outside was reassuringly solid and real and unperturbed. The shadow of the pyramid undulated across the lawns and pathways and the smaller buildings, rising sharply to an apex several hundred metres away on the edge of an ornamental lake.

''Can we change the pattern of events taking place in a stratum of spacetime on the other side of the matter/antimatter interface?''

''I believe we can,'' Karve said. The assertion in his tone made up for the lack of confidence he actually felt. ''Probability is the key factor. Any given set of events lead not just in one specific direction but in several probable directions. Their eventual outcome is not fixed by destiny, only by the law of statistical probability. When we toss a coin we can't say for certain whether it will land heads or tails; what we *can* say is that the probability of either one happening is precisely fifty-fifty.''

''So you want me to project myself into this other 'psi world' or whatever we care to call it?''

Karve raised his head and smiled, rather bleakly. ''I'm asking you to become the anti-matter man,'' he said.

6

U235

Obersalzberg, April 1943

However much one detests Bormann it has to be admitted (and I'm never one to withhold praise where praise is due) that he has done a splendid job with the Führer's Bergof residence. The setting is magnificent. From the balcony the panorama of mountains, valleys and lakes quite literally takes the breath away, and the air is so clear that it is possible to see pleasure steamers on one of the far-distant lakes, at least ten kilometres away. The climate must be good for the Führer and can do nothing but improve his health, which has been wretched these last few months. It has been a worry to me, I must confess, and I have it in mind to concoct some new preparations to prevent further deterioration in his condition. The Ultraseptyl—even a 250 mg. dose twice daily—doesn't seem to perk him up as it used to; it would seem something stronger is required.

Speaking of Bormann, he's been tremendously active recently, poking his nose here, there and everywhere. Hardly surprising, I suppose, since he had that remarkable piece of good fortune when Hess flew to Leningrad in '41 on some madcap scheme or other. This left our friend Martin in the happy position of being next in line as head of the Party Chancellery, and I know for a fact that Goering was incensed at this and repeatedly warned the Führer about him, but wooden balls chose to ignore the advice as usual. Now Goering and Bormann detest each other almost as much as I detest the pair of them. What bothers Fatty Hermann, of course, is that Bormann might supersede him as next in succession to the Führer: with Bormann living in Hitler's pocket, so to speak (he even keeps the same ridiculous working hours, 2 p.m.–5a.m.) and Goering always away in Karinhall, his country palace in the Schorfheide, the fear is by no means groundless. I'm watching developments with interest.

Yesterday morning (Sunday) we went for a walk down to the village. There were seven of us in the party including a personal bodyguard to the Führer, SS Hauptsturmführer Bornholdt, a member of the special SS security guard, Führerbegleitkommando. The locals can never get over seeing Hitler strolling about (perhaps hobbling would be a more accurate description) without a heavily-armed escort. He must seem to them like a god descending from Mount Olympus, this legendary figure from on high hobnobbing with mere mortals. Naturally they've seen him often enough before, but always in newsreels on grand state occasions, surrounded by thousands of people, or visiting troops at the Front, patting the heads of the sick and wounded. One old fellow yesterday actually got down on his knees in the dirt as if to receive a saintly benediction, and our gracious Führer limped over and touched the man's bowed head. We were all deeply moved.

Eva dawdled a little so that the two of us were some distance behind the main party and asked in a low voice why I hadn't been to her room recently. She was, she said, "dying for it," and I had to point out that with Bormann hovering around, his black molelike eyes alert to everything, we had to be extra careful. "He only needs a hint of the slightest impropriety," I told her, "and he'll be slithering in to the Führer and spreading evil rumours about us. He has to leave soon for Berlin, and then. . ."

I let my hand fall casually behind and gripped her buttocks, giving the meaty swell a good hard squeeze. It will be enough to keep her going a while longer.

Felix reports that the difficulties experienced with transportation of supplies have now been overcome—and not before time. It was particularly galling that they should arise just when production of Vitachocs had reached one million units per week. They were being stockpiled in the factory at an alarming rate and the Military in Budapest were refusing point-blank to provide the necessary rolling-stock to ship them out, making the tame excuse that armaments en route for the North Africa campaign had to be given priority. This was an intolerable state of affairs and might have seriously jeopardized our projected target figures for the year; therefore a quiet word in the Führer's ear was called for.

I recall that at the time he had been suffering from a severe attack of stomach cramp accompanied by almost continual migraine, so I prescribed an increased dosage of Dr Koester's Antigas Pills, from twelve up to eighteen tablets daily, and in addition to the usual injections a further six injections of dextrose, hormones and vitamins in variable quantities. It was my belief that sooner or later we would strike a happy balance. The final injection of the day, at ten o'clock, was the heaviest, so that he was usually fairly groggy for an hour or so, and it was then I happened to mention that supplies were becoming more and more difficult to obtain. When he demanded to know why, I told him that the Military was withholding shipments and he at once issued a Personal Directive, dictated to Gertraud Junge (firm body and substantial thighs) to the effect that supplies from the factory in Budapest were to be given priority over and above all war materiel.

This decision, I later learned, angered General Jodl, but of course he was powerless to do anything about it. "Loyal sons of the Reich are laying down their lives in the desert wastes of Africa," the old buffoon was reported as saying, "and our vital transportation links are given over to bars of chocolate!"

Felix is also pleased at the success of the "Russia" lice-powder since it was made compulsory for all the armed forces. Demand now exceeds supply several times over and he is busy recruiting new labour, taking the healthiest and strongest women from local concentration camps. In his last letter he interjects a little joke: "Very handy, dear Theo, to be able to treat the workers with the product they are making—saves a great deal of time and expense." I had to grin when I read it.

So all in all things are progressing most satisfactorily. Some busybody academics at Leipzig University tried to cause a fuss by saying that our patented sulphonamide, Ultraseptyl, was harmful to the nervous system, but the so-called "proof" they came up with didn't convince me—nor the Führer when he read it. These academics are nothing but charlatans; they haven't a clue when it comes to treating actual patients. It was just the same when I invented penicillin: the American Secret Service stole the formula and passed it on to one of their universities who published the research before I could get round to it. I still fume about that every time I think of it.

Anyway, the academics could do nothing to halt production of Ultraseptyl which is now, so I'm told, the leading product of its kind in Germany. Things are happening so quickly that it's difficult to keep track of my personal wealth; my income must be approaching ten thousand marks a month, though I don't know the exact figure. One day I must add it all up and see how much I'm worth.

News from the various battle zones has been mixed these past few weeks. The British 8th Army, under Montgomery, has met with an unexpected setback in West Africa. The Nippon-American force commanded by Patton made a series of night landings on the coast and formed a pincer movement which split the British force, and the worst of it was that the forward battery of 18-pounders was separated from the munitions convoy, some thirty kilometres to the north. Montgomery had no alternative but to withdraw his support troops and leave the artillery to face the enemy alone. The most recent report says that 150 were killed or wounded and over 400 taken prisoner. It was not a happy day when the Führer received that particular dispatch.

For obvious reasons the news disseminated by the newspapers and over the wireless bears little or no relation to the truth. When the reports from the various fronts are gloomy or depressing they are either totally suppressed or altered to such an extent that what has been a defeat is made to seem a victory; or if the news is good it is amplified and exaggerated so that what might have been a routine military operation appears as yet another victory for the great and glorious Third Reich. This is Goebbels' genius: he has a total stranglehold on every organ of mass communication and is so adept at patriotic speeches which rally the nation whenever there is the slightest cause for concern over public morale. My admiration for his skill knows no bounds.

Talking with Willi Johannmeier, Wehrmachtattaché to the Führer, about this very subject the other day and he remarked that if the Proletariat ever learned about the débâcle in Yugoslavia last summer there would be a real stink. Nothing at all leaked out about the episode—not a single word—despite the fact that we lost several divisions, both German and British, three Panzer corps, and Rommel himself admitted that the Yugoslav partisans in the mountains were a match for any army, however well trained, equipped and led.

I confessed to him that I had never understood how Goebbels had managed to cover up the defeat so successfully; after all, wouldn't the survivors talk about it on their return home? It needed just one soldier to reveal the truth and the "rumour" would spread like wildfire.

Willi smiled in that calm, lazy manner which, were one not careful, could deceive by its gentleness, and asked me had I ever heard of the Werewolves. I had heard of them but that was about the sum of it.

"They are commanded by SS Obergruppenführer Hans Pruetzmann," said Willi. "After the Yugoslavian campaign he was ordered by the Reichsführer to detain every last soldier, wounded or not, and to hold them at a camp near

Modra, a small town to the north of Bratislava."

I must have reacted visibly to this because Willi said, his smile intact, "No, no, Theo, they were not exterminated. Crack fighting troops are too valuable to feed into the ovens."

"Then what was the reason?"

"Pruetzmann held them at the camp for two weeks' intensive indoctrination. He didn't try to fool them into believing the defeat had never happened—no, he was much more subtle than that. In fact his instructions were explicitly the reverse."

"From Himmler?"

Willi nodded, his eyes lazy with amusement. "Pruetzmann had a comprehensive and detailed dossier on the families of every man there: wives, sons, daughters, mothers, fathers, brothers, sisters, grandparents, aunts, uncles, cousins. He told them a dozen times each day, every day for two weeks, that if one word got out concerning what had actually happened during the Yugoslavian campaign the Werewolves would attend to the lot of them—eliminate every relative down to the last babe-in-arms. They believed him too, and well they should, for he was deadly serious."

"The Werewolves are trained assassins, I take it."

"An underground organization," Willi confirmed. "Their original purpose was to organize a German resistance movement should we be occupied by foreign invaders, but of course the Führer will not entertain such a notion for an instant. Therefore the Werewolves had to be found a new role." He paused and drew on his fat cigar, leaning back in his chair, comfortably at ease. "A little story which might amuse you. You've met SS Brigadeführer Walter Schellenberg, Head of RSHA Amt VI, I believe? He was given the task of forwarding, via Himmler, a confidential report compiled by Major-General Gehlen on the Polish underground movement. It contained some useful ideas on how one should go about organizing such a movement if it seemed necessary. Well, Schellenberg submitted the report personally and waited while Himmler read it."

Willi's face creased into a smile.

"The Reichsführer went berserk. 'This is complete and utter madness!' he shouted. 'If I were to discuss such a plan with General Wenck I should be denounced as the first defeatist in the Third Reich. The fact would be served up to the Führer piping hot!' Poor Walter. Filled with such good intentions that always seem to go wrong."

Yet it was evident that Willi revelled in poor Walter's discomfiture, not even bothering to hide his delight. I reflected, looking at Willi, how cautious one has to be, even (or especially!) with one's closest associates; not one of them would hesitate to stab his dearest friend in the back if there was anything to be gained by it.

We moved on to talk of other matters. Willi was unrelievedly gloomy about the spring offensive in the Far East. "The British can't fight the Japanese," was his opinion. "They're too much the gentlemen playing a jolly game of cricket. The Japanese have their code of honour too, but it doesn't prevent them butchering the Filipinos. Do you know, Theo," he said, looking at me keenly through the cigar smoke, "I sometimes wonder what it would have been like to have had the Japanese as allies instead of the British. The Japs believe in total war too, you know. *Weltmacht oder Niedergang**."

"You think Mandrake has let us down?" I asked, watching him carefully.

"No, not Mandrake himself. The British people. They've no heart for this fight. No stomach for it either. They'd never have ventured so far east if it hadn't been for Australia and New Zealand."

"It's a difficult war out there. The conditions aren't what they're used to. Now in France and the Low Countries their rule is strict and absolute. Their invasion went even more smoothly than ours when we took Poland."

"What days those were," Willi said dreamily, a rapt smile encapsulating his cigar. "That was the Reich at its best, the

*World domination or ruin.

flower of German manhood in full bloom. 'Our finest hour,' as Mandrake said."

"It was a brilliant speech," I agreed. "A graceful compliment."

"Do you think the Allies will win?" he asked abruptly, gazing at the ceiling as if the question was of no consequence.

I considered my reply. "I think America is the stumbling-block. They're not yet fully committed to the war effort. If they decide on complete mobilization then the Allies could be up against it. We need to strike *at* them, not wait for them to come to us."

"True, true." Willi lowered his head and glanced round the room. "You're closer to the Führer's privileged circle than I am."

"I'd hardly say that," I smiled modestly.

"Come now, Theo, you know it's true." He lowered his voice. "Have you heard any talk of a secret weapon? A wonder weapon? Something that could be used to knock both Russia and America out of the war at a single stroke?"

I gazed at him without, I hoped, any expression. Was he testing me? Was there some doubt as to my political loyalty? This would need delicate handling. "Not a wonder weapon as such," I replied ambiguously.

"But you have heard of *U235*?"

"Oh that," I said. "Oh yes."

"It hasn't even been mentioned in conference yet—ultra top secret known to just a select few. Christian put me wise."

"Christian?"

"Eckard. Chef Luftwaffenführungsstab."

"Oh yes."

"The scientists are almost at the stage where they are ready to test it. Apparently—I find this impossible to believe, quite frankly—they say it will decimate an area *ten thousand kilometres square*."

"That's what I heard too."

"Can you imagine it?" He waved his cigar in the air. "With a device like that we could wipe out Moscow, Leningrad, New York, Washington, San Francisco, Tokyo. . ."

He became lost in dreadful contemplation, a small bemused smile on his lips.

"How big is it, this device?"

"No idea," Willi said. "Not a clue. Eckard says it contains some kind of new material, very unstable stuff by all accounts. That's what they call *U235*. But how it works and what the actual device is like he couldn't say."

"An area ten thousand kilometres square."

"Tremendous, eh? That'd teach 'em who was boss."

"And we're almost ready to test it?"

"Later this year. They've selected the Ukraine as the site. Wipe out a few million more peasants. My God, they'll wonder what's hit them." He emitted a little squeak of amusement and choked on the cigar smoke.

"Probably why they call it the wonder weapon," I said, punching his arm.

20th April, a great celebration: the Führer's birthday!

Unfortunately he wasn't feeling very well and we had to curtail the festivities. An informal party for about fourteen people had been arranged, to take place during the afternoon, but when I attended him shortly after 2 p.m. he was in a dreadful state. His left arm and left leg were shaking uncontrollably and when he rose to his feet his stoop was even more pronounced than usual. He complained of a headache and said that his vision was affected; there was also a strange pallor to his skin, like a mottled grey. Most odd.

Immediately I prepared a triple injection: 200 mg. of Amylobarbitone to calm the nervous system, 60 mg. of a para-sympatholytic (Hyoscyamine) to relieve the tremors in his limbs, followed by 6 mg. of Picrotoxin to act as a stimulant.

He became lethargic for half an hour, went into convulsions (probably the effect of the Picrotoxin) and then revived and seemed to be his old self once more. It was important that he look fit and healthy because Goebbels had sent a film camera team along to take some newsreels of the Führer on the balcony, enjoying his birthday celebration. By about three-thirty he was able to stand and walk unaided, so we went outdoors and Hitler played with Blondi, making a great fuss over his Alsatian. Eva had put on (at my insistence) a bathing costume and we frolicked about for twenty minutes or so for the benefit of the camera.

In a brief respite later on, standing by the rail and pretending to be drinking in the marvellous alpine scenery, I asked Eva what she had heard of this device known as *U235*. She said that it had been mentioned but that was all, and I told her to find out everything she could about it.

Obersalzberg, May 1943
More meddling interference from Brandt and his cronies. "We are concerned," they write in a memorandum, "for the health of the Führer. His general demeanour we find disturbing and we think it advisable to meet with yourself and discuss in some precise detail the medication you are prescribing."

It is signed Dr. Karl Brandt, Begleitarzt (Surgeon to the Führer); Dr. Hans Karl von Hasselbach, Deputy Surgeon; Dr. Erwin Giesing, E.N.T. Specialist.

If the idiots think I am going to allow them to step in now, after all these years, and make a mess of all I've worked for, the careful planning, the scrupulous diagnostic case-work, the hours of preparing new compounds and mixtures—if they really believe I am going to stand aside and let them queer the pitch they must be out of their heads.

Himmler arrived this morning bearing more bad news. As if the North African and Middle East campaigns weren't going disastrously enough, the Reichsführer now brings word that the anticipated breakthrough on the Eastern Front hasn't materialized and isn't likely to in the foreseeable future. The Russian forward position ("the thin red line," as Himmler remarked of it contemptuously), when just on the point of breaking, received American and Japanese reinforcements; not a large force, so it appears, but they were equipped with the new GM tanks and Mitishubi armaments. The result—stalemate.

I wasn't present when the news was given to the Führer but I heard later that he was speechless, eyes bulging, foaming at the mouth, and he had another bout of the twitches. This from Julius, two keeps me informed of everything that goes on during my absence.

The strategic dilemma, it seems, is that the Allied General Staff is very much afraid that if a breakthrough isn't made during the summer months the fierce Russian winter will bog down the troops of both sides till the spring of '44 at the earliest. The Führer will not stand for this and Himmler's mission is to agree an immediate strategy and carry the decision posthaste to Field-Marshal Reichenau. However, I very much doubt whether Hitler is in sufficient possession of his faculties to make any kind of rational appraisement of the situation; nor is he able to form a workable or even coherent plan of action.

Julius also mentioned that, during his audience with the Führer, Himmler broached the subject of a special squad, to be known as the SS HADER Unit, whose purpose, as near as I can make out, is to create discord and strife amongst the civilian population of occupied territories. Why it is necessary to do this I haven't a notion, unless the Reichsführer believes it will hinder their resistance movements. It wouldn't surprise me to learn that the idea emanated from Wulf, Himmler's personal astrologer, who has a strong influence on all his decisions.

I haven't confided this to anyone, not even to Eva, but the behaviour of many of the high-ranking officers seems to me of late to be verging on the lunatic. They are more concerned with building their own little empires than with trying to win the war. At this rate it will drag on for years and might even lead to the unthinkable possibility of defeat for the Third Reich.

Felix and I have discussed this matter before, on several occasions, but I think it might be advisable in the very near future to open an account in Switzerland. Should the worst happen and all assets are frozen it would be foolish to be left holding millions of marks which wouldn't be worth the paper they're printed on. The plan would entail a discreet transfer of capital to Switzerland, buy gold, deposit it in a numbered account, and make preparations for a speedy departure.

I shall inform Felix of my intention without delay. One never knows.

Another disturbed night: they seem to be occurring much more frequently now.

I had settled down with a good book, a nightcap, and a box of my own special brand, and after reading for about an hour was drifting off into a beautifully relaxed sleep when my bedside telephone started ringing. It was Heinz Linge, the Führer's manservant. He told me to come at once and tend to the Führer who had, in his phrase, "gone cuckoo." I put my dressing-gown on, picked up my bag, and hurried along to the Führer's private apartments on the floor above.

The bedchamber was in a frightful mess. The dressing-table had been swept clean, there were bottles and jars all over the floor, including several vials of Dr. Koester's Antigas Pills; the wall drapes had been torn from their fitments, and one of the wardrobe doors had all but been wrenched from its hinges. The large ornamental mirror of Venetian glass had a splintered crack from top to bottom and all the lightshades were askew.

The Führer was standing amidst the debris, arms taut at his sides, fists clenched, eyes fixed as in a trance on some distant non-existent object. He was wearing pyjamas and a silk dressing-gown embroidered with his initials, one letter on each lapel in large gothic script.

Although my attention was on him I caught the fleeting impression of Eva's white strained face amongst the crumpled bedclothes, tear-streaked, watching me with a kind of dumb terrified pleading. I motioned to her to remain calm and stepped up quietly behind the Führer.

He seemed to be in the grip of a catatonic brainstorm, totally rigid except for his jowls which were quivering and his nostrils flaring and closing, the harsh breath rasping in his throat.

This requires careful handling, I thought to myself. He doesn't seem very well, probably a tummy upset; the news from the Eastern Front must have disturbed his gastric juices. However, I have seen him suddenly lash out on such occasions, blindly, completely oblivious to his surroundings, and I didn't want to receive a black eye or a broken jaw for my pains.

"Are you all right, mein armes, krankes Kälbchen?"*

His breathing faltered at this familiar phrase and he whimpered a little down his nose. I put both hands on his shoulders and gently pushed him towards a chair. He sank down into it, I could feel his body trembling, and it was as though someone had released the strings on a puppet and the tiny wooden limbs and tiny wooden head are slackly at rest.

"Have you had the visions?" I asked, taking his limp wrist and feeling for the pulse. "Have they been troubling you again?"

He stirred and lifted his head a fraction, apparently seeing me for the first time; the dull blue-grey eyes hardened into focus, the lips moved, the moustache twitched, and he said:

"I couldn't get it up."

"Get what up?"

He made a weary indication with his head in the direction of the bed.

"Well, you *are* a bad boy," I said. "I gave you some tablets for that, don't you remember? And some ointment to rub on it." I released his arm and it flopped into his lap.

"I took the tablets and used the ointment but they didn't work. I just felt dizzy. What am I to do, Theo? I can't do the trick. I want to but I can't."

"Now, now, don't upset yourself." I glanced over his head at Eva and she was making a strangling gesture with

*My poor sick calf.

both hands round an invisible throat and miming instructions to go with it. I cautioned her with a slight gesture and she stuck her tongue out at me.

"Is it the spirits, do you think?" he asked in a low voice. "You told me that the spirits of the body sometimes get angry and take their revenge by disobeying the owner's wishes." He was looking at me beseechingly.

"That might be the reason. It's very complicated. It might be the spirits but it could well be the signs. Have you studied the omens recently? If the omens are not propitious it's possible that the spirits of the body are fighting amongst themselves. The juxtapositions are all-important."

He sighed heavily. "I wish I understood it more clearly. Where did you learn all these things, Theo?"

"It took many, many years to become an adept. I studied the mystical chronicles and drank deeply at the well of ancient wisdom. It is a gift, this understanding, not given to many."

"What would I do without you, Theo? All the rest are vermin. They think they can fool me with their degrees and their paper qualifications. But they couldn't even relieve me of the cramps."

I sat down in the chair opposite and took his hands in mine. "Dismiss them from your thoughts, süsses, armes Kindchen* Adolf. If they had their way they would butcher you—slit you open and poke around inside. Why, only the other day von Hasselbach—" I checked myself. "Not that it matters. Let us forget it."

"Forget what?" he said, his body stiffening.

"Never mind, it isn't important. In any case they don't really mean it."

"What don't they really mean?" His hands were clammy and cold in mine. "What is it, Theo? What have they been saying about me?"

I raised my eyebrows. "If you must know, mein Führer, if you insist on dragging it out of me. . ."

*Poor sweet baby.

"Yes. Yes. I do. What is it?"

"They say you have Parkinson's disease."

He looked at me thunderously. "They dare say that? Those quacks, those cretins say I have a *disease?* I have never met the man. Whose son is he? Have I met him? Is it contagious?"

"Whose son do you mean?" I asked.

"Parkin's."

"No, you misunderstand, Liebchen. The disease is called *Parkinson's*. It is a nervous complaint."

His lips were working, his jaw thrust forward pugnaciously. "Nervous?"

"Otherwise known as shaking palsy."

His eyes bulged and the veins in his neck stood out. His hands, held within mine, were like claws. He tried to speak but the words were strangled in his throat.

"Characterized by rigidity of the facial muscles," I added.

Tiny specks of foam escaped his lips. His left eye developed a nervous tic. He tried again to speak but nothing came out.

"It produces, so they say, a mask-like expression," I informed him. "There's also muscle weakness which leads to a peculiar stooping gait. It's a disease usually associated with people approaching old age, caused by deterioration of the brain cells."

"*Urglhhmaaach!*" went Hitler.

"I'll read you the full definition if you like," I said, reaching for my bag. "I have a medical dictionary with me."

His head moved jerkily to and fro in what I took to be a negative reaction.

"You'd better give him something, Theo," Eva said. "He's about to have another fit."

"Not yet, I want him to remain conscious. I can't talk to him if he's flat out."

I patted his hand and made soothing noises for a few minutes and gradually he regained control of his motor functions. A semblance of colour returned to his face, though once again I noticed the peculiar discoloration of the skin:

blotches of sickly pasty grey on his cheeks and forehead. I must give him some calamine for that, I remember thinking.

When he had recovered I led him back to bed and tucked him in. "Don't worry your head about von Hasselbach and the other quacks," I said. "While I'm here nobody will harm you."

Eva looked at me and then raised her eyes to the ceiling in mute despair.

I said, "We shall have to consult the signs and omens. The spirits of the body are unsettled; they are unhappy."

"I only wanted to get it up."

"I know, I know," I placated him. "Quite natural. When was the last time it was hard? That you can remember."

Hitler gazed into the room and after a moment's hesitation said, "Don't know," somewhat sulkily, and I thought I saw a tear in his eye.

I sat down at the bedside and stroked the silken sleeve of his dressing-gown. "Listen. I have some new stuff that's supposed to work wonders. It's been tested on captured Russian airmen and the reports up to now have been very favourable."

He turned to look at me, one eye obscured by a lock of greasy black hair. "Will it do the trick?" he asked morosely.

I grinned. "Eva will be able to answer that for you," and reached down into my bag. "It's a tincture of strychnine, a mild variety, you understand. No harmful side-effects."

It was true about the Russian airmen: they were kept in tanks of freezing water for six hours and then put into bed with two Jewish whores. They had a problem similar to the Führer's (though the cause was somewhat different) and were given strychnine to stimulate the respiratory and cardiovascular centres. It worked too—though in one or two cases the drug caused tremors and convulsions and eventually death from respiratory paralysis. I didn't want to alarm him unnecessarily and I omitted to mention the tedious details.

He took 8 mg. orally and we awaited results.

Eva lay propped on one elbow, an expression of absolute

deadening boredom on her face. She wrinkled her nose at me and crossed her eyes. I made a funny face back at her. With her eyes she signalled *Will it send him to sleep?* I raised my eyebrows to indicate that I hadn't the faintest idea, whereupon she sighed and pulled down the corners of her mouth. I let my eyes drift from her face down to her nightgown: through the flimsy material I could see the vague dark ovals of her nipples. She noticed the direction of my gaze and lowered her eyes, glancing at me through her lashes and licking her bottom lip with a soft pink tongue.

For some time now I hadn't found her in the least desirable, but this simple stratagem rekindled my interest and I took it into my head to have a poke at it at the next opportunity.

"How do you feel?" I asked the Führer. "Anything stirring?"

His eyes were glazed and it occurred to me that perhaps the dose had been too strong. On reading the label carefully I found that it prescribed a gradual increase from 2 mg. to 8 mg. over a period of days. Well, it was too late now. No good crying over spilt strychnine.

"I don't feel to be here," he said, and indeed his voice did sound odd. "I feel to be. . ."

"Anywhere in particular?"

"I think I can see God."

"Oh mother," said Eva.

"You can see God," I said. "That's interesting."

Eva tapped her temple with her forefinger and pointed at Hitler. I nodded and murmured, "As a hatter."

"What?" the Führer said, blinking rapidly and trying to sit up.

"Take it easy now. No cause for alarm. Can you see anyone else besides God? Any angels? Visions?"

He has often mentioned to me, in confidence, that he receives "visitations." Sometimes there are ghosts present, and once he said that he could see right through me and tried to poke his finger into my chest until I insisted that I was perfectly real and solid and what's more he was hurting me.

I leaned closer and said in his ear, "Can you feel anything yet, Messiah of the Reich? Is anything twitching down below? Is the little worm coming out of its nest?"

"Oh bollocks," Eva said impatiently, "let me have a feel." She rummaged under the bedclothes.

"Anything?"

"Not a sausage."

"I must have given him too much."

"You didn't give him enough."

"It would have killed him."

"Exactly."

"The visions, the visions. . ." mumbled the Führer.

"Yes, the bleeding visions," I said.

"They're speaking to me, giving me instructions."

"Ask them if they can give you a hard on."

"I shall rule the world with my wonder weapon," he burbled.

"And pigs might fly," Eva said.

"Quiet," I said. "This could be interesting. Which wonder weapon are you referring to, mein Führer?"

"The most powerful weapon on earth."

Eva had another feel. "He really is delirious."

"Shush."

"I have not come into the world to make men better but to make use of their weaknesses," he droned. "Now I have the means. Total annihilation. The skies will darken, the bombs will rain down on the cities, blood will flow in the gutters. Nature is cruel, therefore we too may be cruel. If I can send the flower of the German nation into the hell of war, without the smallest pity for the spilling of precious German blood, then surely I have a right to remove millions of an inferior race that breeds like vermin!"

"How will this be achieved, mein Liebling?" I asked softly.

"The ultimate weapon," Hitler gloated, his blank eyes lost in visions. "The brilliance of German science and technology has given the Reich the miracle of *U235*. Now nothing on earth can stand in our way. We are truly invincible. The visions tell me of greater glories ahead. I see, I believe, I will act. God wills it."

"And we have it—the most powerful weapon on earth?"

"Yes, yes," Hitler breathed, his eyes alight with phantoms. "We have it. The Atomic Bomb."

Obersalzberg, June 1943

This must surely be the loveliest time of the year. Difficult to believe, here amidst this idyllic alpine landscape, that throughout Europe, Russia, Africa, the Middle East, the Far East, the Pacific, on every continent and ocean, bloody battles are being fought and men, women and children are dying in the most sordid inglorious circumstances. Life is funny that way, I suppose. Some must die so that others might live. So it goes.

Goebbels paid a brief visit to the Berghof. He didn't look at all well and wasn't, I might add, in the best of moods. Indeed he took the Führer to task for not putting in an appearance in Berlin for over two months. The gist of his complaint was that the German people were having to suffer an increasing aerial bombardment by the Americans and the Russians, cities and towns were being knocked flat, and yet the Führer hadn't once visited the devastated areas to bring cheer and comfort to those living under daily threat to their lives. Goebbels himself, as is well known, is constantly touring the industrialized areas on morale-boosting missions; cculdn't the Führer, if only for propaganda purposes, leave Obersalzberg and see at first-hand the destruction that was being inflicted? The German people would respond magnificently if they saw the Führer taking a close personal interest.

Hitler was taking tea at the time of the interview. He had, as I recall, just eaten a cream bun and was licking the cream from his fingers. He looked at Goebbels with that fixed unwavering gaze of his, the blue-grey eyes staring and dead, lacking animation, like those of a somnambulist.

"The bomb-terror," he declared, "spares the dwellings of neither rich nor poor; before the offices of total war the last class barriers have had to go down. Under the debris of our shattered cities the last so-called achievements of the middle-class nineteenth century have been finally buried."

Goebbels started to interrupt but the Führer cried:

"There is no end to the revolution! A revolution is only doomed to failure if those who make it cease to be revolutionaries. Together with the monuments of bourgeois culture there crumble also the last obstacles to the fulfilment of our revolutionary task. Now that everything is in ruins we are forced to rebuild Europe. In the past, private possessions imprisoned us in the class structure: now the bombs, instead of killing all Europeans, have only smashed the prison walls which held them captive. In trying to destroy Europe's future the enemy has only succeeded in smashing its past; and with that, everything old and outworn has gone. Gone for evermore."

Several of us applauded this speech and the Führer looked up as if awakening from a trance, and Goebbels sat sullen and stiff, his hands sunk deeply in the pockets of his black leather greatcoat.

"Is this the message I have to take back with me?" he asked. I have never seen him so depressed and spiritless, bereft of all hope.

"Tell them to trust in the Führer and in the stars. It is written in my horoscope that the second half of the year will be the turning-point for us. This is June the eleventh. It is the turning-point!"

At this Goebbels stood up abruptly and begged to be excused. He left immediately for Berlin accompanied by his adjutant SS Hauptsturmführer Guenther Schwaegermann and other personal aides.

At last I have found someone who talks sense about this mysterious substance *U235*, the vital constituent of the "Atomic Bomb."

An officer arrived at the Berghof bringing a confidential dispatch for the Führer, and after discharging his duty, spent an hour or so relaxing on the balcony in the hot sunshine: it was there we struck up a casual conversation. A young man, mid-twenties I should say, close-cropped sandy-coloured hair, an over-eagerness of speech which made him stutter.

Nicolaus von Below, Wehrmachtattaché (Luftwaffe) to Goering, acting as liaison officer to the Führer's headquarters. I had no idea what the dispatch contained but happened to remark that it must have been of vital importance if the authorities had to employ the services of an Oberst der Luftwaffe.

"It concerns the B-B-Bomb," said von Below, rather rashly I thought, not knowing what my security clearance was. "Of course you are familiar with the project, being so c-c-close to the Führer."

"*U235*," I said knowledgeably.

"It will win the war for us. Neither the Soviets, the Americans nor the Japanese have anything like it. In a year from n-n-now—all over."

"Why a year?"

"The process is extremely complex," said von Below, and went on to explain that *U235* is composed of the lighter atoms of natural uranium. A team of physicists, working under the direction of Professor Max Steenback, has developed a very high speed centrifuge which separates these lighter atoms from the rest, eventually producing what he termed "enriched uranium." This 2-4 per cent concentration of active uranium is then incorporated in a device which, when triggered, has the explosive power of 100,000 tons of TNT.

"They call it a chain-reaction. When the *U235* has reached the right level of c-c-concentration something known as fission takes place—the atoms go out of control and the result is a m-m-massive explosion."

"Staggering," I said, shaking my head in wonderment and admiration. "This proves once and for all the invincible superiority of German technology."

"It is a new era," von Below confirmed with shining eyes. "The Atomic Age. Nothing known to m-m-man can stand in its way. There is no defence against it. The Reich will triumph. Historical N-N-Necessity and Justice will prevail in the end!"

In answer to my questions he informed me that the device, though large, could be carried quite easily by heavy bomber and dropped from 25,000 metres on to the target. At approximately 1,000 metres the Bomb would be detonated by a built-in automatic altimeter system. I expressed surprise at this and von Below explained, "It is detonated in the air to achieve m-m-maximum effect. In addition to the heat-blast the Bomb spreads a form of radiation which will give the enemy population skin cancer. And this isn't all—" he was becoming more and more agitated "—the radiation sickness will last through m-m-many generations. Babies in the womb will be born deformed, with no arms and legs and with shrunken b-b-bodies. The sperm and egg-cells of those who survive will c-c-carry the sickness so that their offspring will be mutants too—laughable parodies of human beings."

I was very impressed with Nicolaus von Below: his boyish enthusiasm and unwavering loyalty to the Reich are qualities not in abundant supply at the present time and which many could do worse than emulate, especially those in positions of high command. My only criticism is that he might have been more circumspect in his handling of top secret information; not everyone is trustworthy, even amongst those (sad to say) who are privy to the Führer's most intimate confidences.

If victory is sweet, revenge is sweeter.

This observation is prompted by a feeling of secret bubbling exultation. This morning, shortly after eleven o'clock, a "deputation" arrived without warning: Brandt, Giesing and von Hasselbach on a mission which had quite obviously been planned weeks ahead and down to the smallest detail.

The appointment had been made, it transpired, through administrative network of the security guard, Reichssicherheitsdienst Dienststelle I. The first I knew of it was when Heinz Linge called me in great alarm and said that Giesing had been poking around in the medicine cabinet and discovered several cartons of Dr. Koester's Antigas Pills and had demanded to know what in heaven's name these were for. Heinz had said (he was flustered) that they were part of the Führer's personal medication as prescribed by me, whereupon Giesing turned pale and rushed out of the room.

I sensed immediately that something was afoot and went directly to the ante-room of Hitler's private apartment. Julius informed me that the three doctors were in consultation with the Führer and that I would be well advised, under the circumstances, not to intervene unless summoned. I reminded him of his pledge to me, on behalf of the Führer and the Fatherland, he had given five years before at the Reich Chancellery in Berlin. I went on:

"You have seen for yourself the precarious hold he has on life; do you think those butchers have the faintest inkling of the delicate nature of his constitution? It is our right and our duty to protect him from the blundering interference of such meddlesome quacks."

Just then (destiny smiles on the audacious) the buzzer sounded, summoning Julius inside, and I unhesitatingly followed, to be greeted by thunderous scowls on the faces of the three doctors.

The Führer was sitting at his desk, leaning slightly to one side, his chin resting in the palm of his hand, smoking a cigarette in a holder, a haze of blue smoke obscuring his head.

There was a lengthy silence which no one seemed keen to interrupt; Julius stood attentively by, awaiting instructions. I surmised that someone had finished speaking the moment we entered—von Hasselbach I gathered, judging from his flushed appearance and fidgety manner.

At last the Führer spoke, a voice issuing from the pall of blue smoke. "I was about to send for you, Theo. I have just this minute heard the most remarkable thing. Would you like to hear what it is?"

"Certainly, mein Führer, if you think it concerns me."

"I think it does; wouldn't you say so, Herr Doktor Brandt?"

Brandt had been glaring at me but now he seemed taken aback. "Why, yes, of course—of course—" He was plainly confused.

"These three wise men," said the voice in the smoke, "these three learned physicians inform me that I am being slowly and systematically poisoned. What do you think of that?"

I looked at them one by one. "Is that what they say?"

"Not in that way precisely," said von Hasselbach. "What we were saying was that, in our opinion—"

"Did I invite you to speak?" the Führer said. A billow of blue smoke rolled ominously across the desk like a thundercloud.

"Forgive me. I wasn't thinking. My abject apoligies."

More silence.

"How long have you been attending me, Theo?"

"Seven years, nearly eight, mein Führer."

"Have I suffered one head cold in all that time?"

"No, mein Führer."

"Have I been admitted to hospital in all that time?"

"No, mein Führer."

"Have you diagnosed any disease or infection during those seven years?"

"Except for a mild complaint of the inner ear, no, mein Führer."

"If I may be allowed, sir, to interject at this point," Giesing spoke up. "We—"

"Shut up!" Hitler screamed. "Shut up! Shut up! You dolts! You cretins! You imbecilic swine! Do you think I'm an idiot? Do you think I'm not familiar with your charlatan's tricks? You think I have a disease—*don't deny it*—I can see it in your faces. You believe, all three of you, that I'm suffering from some nervous disorder. Don't deny it! *Don't deny it!* For four years I have directed a war on a global scale. I am the greatest military strategist of all time, and yet you in your infinite quackery think my health is impaired. What understanding do you have of political affairs? None! What do you know of military matters? Nothing! Yet you blunder in here and try to tell me—*me!*—that I am being poisoned, that my judgment is at fault, that I have lost all control."

Brandt stepped forward.

"Mein Führer, forgive me, we have never for an instant doubted your political or military genius. It is purely on a medical basis that we are concerned for your—"

"Shut up! Shut up! Shut up! Shut up!" He smashed the top of the desk with both fists. Ash cascaded over the lapels of his double-breasted light-grey jacket. He said to Julius, "Am I ill? You see me every day. Am I sickening for anything? Am I nervous? Tell them. Tell them!"

"No, mein Führer." Julius caught my eye and swallowed. "You are not nervous. You are in perfect health."

"You *see*?" Hitler yelled at the top of his voice. "He sees me every day, several times a day, and he says I am in perfect health. Per. Fect. Health!"

Brandt, von Hasselbach and Giesing averted their eyes from him and each other. Silence came down like a shroud.

"Give me a cigarette," the Führer said, and Julius hurried to comply. When it had been inserted in the holder and was going satisfactorily he said, "You are men of paper, you three. Academics. Intellectuals. Out of touch with reality. Morell here is a qualified doctor, just as you three are, but he understands that real medicine isn't concerned simply with flesh and muscle and bone. There are spirits of the body that have to be tended, cared for, treated with respect, and occasionally appeased. What do you know of these spirits? You, Giesing, what do you know?"

Giesing shuffled his feet and tried not to meet anyone's eye. "I know very little about spirits," he admitted. "If you mean the psychological treatment of patients—"

"Psychological!" the Führer bellowed, his eyes protruding from his head. "You dare to mention in my presence the perverted theories of a Jew? You tell me to my face that you subscribe to Jewish methods of treatment? You believe—believe—"

He was incoherent with rage. There was a glazed film over his eyes and his face had broken out in large grey blotches. I thought for a moment he was about to have a seizure.

"What the Führer says is quite correct," I put in quietly. "Modern medicine pays no attention to these all-important spirits. It treats the symptoms but ignores the causes. Unless one understands the dynamic metabolism of the body, the ebb and flow of vital forces, the astrological effects of the spheres on the bodily processes, then medical treatment is of no practical value. You might as well put sticking plaster on a gangrenous leg in order to cure it."

Brandt was gaping at me as though I was talking gibberish. Both von Hasselbach and Giesing had been cowed into stunned silence. My God, they were sorry they'd ever thought of this!

"You, a trained doctor, do not believe in orthodox medical practice?" Brandt said. I cannot accurately describe the expression on his face; it was ludicrous in the extreme.

"You mean the so-called 'body of knowledge' compiled by professors in their academic ivory towers?" I said mockingly. "All those learned old gentlemen with strings of letters after their names? I prefer to trust my own instincts than follow the outdated ramblings of cretinous old fools."

The Führer had regained his composure. He was now icily calm. A shadow had fallen over the room, as of that cast by the outspread wings of a hovering eagle about to swoop down on its prey. He said, his voice under strict control:

"As from today—as of this minute—you are relieved of all medical appointments and political offices. I shall not require your services again, nor your advice, nor do I want any of you admitted into my presence ever again. You are hereby dismissed."

"If victory is sweet," I said to Eva later that day, "revenge is sweeter."

"Don't go on so," she said, pulling my head down. "Kiss me again."

"I'll do more than kiss you," I said, throwing the bed covers out of the way. "I'm going to shaft the arse off you."

7

Brain of the Führer

For what seemed like the *nth* time Queghan compared the RECONPAN report with the Archives' record file and noted yet another inconsistency. He was covered in dust, his throat was parched, and his irritation was mounting. It was so bloody obvious and yet if Pouline deGrenier was such a fool that she couldn't see. . .

He let the thought fade away and die a natural death. Why bother to convince her? The evidence was here for all to see. He didn't need to explain or interpret the facts; the facts spoke eloquently for themselves. But he had tried. He had patiently explained about "projective myths" and the "principles of acausality" and "areas of uncertainty" (it was difficult to discuss Myth Technology without resorting to jargon) and she had closed her eyes and shaken her head as if to say that he might just as well save his breath.

Pouline deGrenier was an intelligent woman with a bright and inquiring mind but she was unable to grasp the infuriating paradox that mythic events could be influenced before and after they had taken place. "Because," Queghan had said, "a mythic event exists in a region of probability. It is at the vortex of human consciousness and experience—a key to the past and the future."

"If it exists it exists," she had replied, not budging an inch. "And if it doesn't it doesn't."

"Then why does the brain in the RECONPAN laboratory insist that in the Second World War Germany and Great

Britain were allies? Why does it talk of the Blackshirt Brigade when there is no historical documentation to show that such a unit ever existed?"

Her candid brown eyes didn't waver from his. "Malfunction," she said crisply.

"That's your explanation?"

"The system is in prototype. I didn't expect one hundred per cent success and I wasn't surprised when the system didn't function properly on experimental trials." She hoped that God, whoever and wherever He was, would forgive her this whopping white lie.

"So now you're going to grow some fresh tissue cultures," Queghan said with a cynical smile.

"Léon is preparing a cyberthetic program to investigate each of the major neurochemical circuits. Within two weeks we should know the results."

Queghan tried another tack. "Doesn't it strike you as odd that all these historical inconsistencies should be so consistent?"

"What do you mean?"

"For all its apparent haphazard selection of data the brain is constructing a valid and plausible mythic experience—it is consistent within its own terms."

"We would expect it to be. If one of the circuits is malfunctioning it will presumably give the same spurious information each time it is triggered. The same with paranoia in human terms: a wave of electrical energy in the brain which habitually follows a particular neuron pathway. Speaking psycho-medically this is what one would expect."

She blocked every tackle, caught every spinning ball he threw at her and deftly tossed it back. And the annoying thing was that in terms of earthbound logic her beliefs were irrefutable. If you chose to deny—as Pouline deGrenier chose to do—the validity of mythic events, of the principle of acausality, of the paradox of probability, then the argument came to an abrupt dead stop. There was no more to be said. In the end they had each stared silently into space and listened to the pressing silence, until eventually Queghan had asked:

"You have no objection to my using the RECONPAN facility?"

"No objection as such."

"What does 'as such' mean?"

"Providing it doesn't interfere with our investigation program."

"You're most generous."

"Not at all."

Now he was determined to prove to this intractable female that the inconsistencies were not the result of malfunction in the system but the accurate projection of mythic events. Yet deep in the labyrinthine entrails of Archives, dust in his eyes and at the back of his throat, Queghan realized the futility of trying to prove anything at all by an endless rote of historical cross-references. To Pouline deGrenier they would have no relevance whatsoever to the main objective of getting RECONPAN to regurgitate slabs of "authentic" history which tallied with official records. She wouldn't be content until Hitler's simulated brain told her precisely and in detail what she already knew.

Queghan replaced the sheets in their vinyl slip-cases and went up to Level 17. With people like Pouline deGrenier there was one way and one way only to prove that the world was round.

When he got home it was 1951 Pre-Colonization. The sleazy woman in the soiled slip said, "Siddown, Polack, and take the weight off."

The groan he uttered was so realistic that she responded instantly by telling him to "Shaddap, punk. I've had enough of your slobbering to last me a lifetime. If you don't like my company, take off."

He said tentatively, "Blanche?"

She halted by the open window just as the harsh green glare of a neon sign gilded her profile, making a fluorescent halo of her blond hair before flickering off and leaving her in silhouette.

"Don't come whining to me, you drunken slob. Where've ya bin till now? I'm working my guts out trying to keep this place together and what do you do? What does he do?" she asked the cracked and flaking plaster ceiling. "I'll tell you what he does: spends every last goddam dime in the bar along the street. I ain't even got a decent pair of shoes to my name."

"Take it easy, Blanche," said Queghan. "No need to get excited."

"Excited! D'ya hear that?" she said to the blistered windowframe. "Me? Excited? Me get excited? What else is there to do around this lousy hole with nothing but a big dumb Polack for company? D'ya want I should thank you or somethin'? D'ya want my gratitude? Am I in your debt?"

"I'm sorry I was late."

"He's sorry," Blanche said, nodding her head and folding her arms. "D'ya hear that?" she inquired of the washbasin in the corner. "How do you like this guy? He walks all over my life and then, calm as you please, tells me he's sorry. How do you like that?"

Queghan took in the period detail and reckoned it was better than the acting. There was traffic in the street below (the sound of traffic) and the wail of a baby from the next tenement. Somebody in the apartment upstairs was brawling with his wife and there was the spasmodic splintering crash of breaking crockery followed by a thickly articulated oath or two.

The room itself was cheap and nasty. The furniture consisted of a ramshackle table and four broken-down chairs, a sagging armchair with the straw stuffing hanging out, a yellow lacquered wardrobe with fiery red roses painted in the corners, and a long mirror inset in the door with a jagged crack across the middle, an iron-framed bed with dented brass knobs at the corners, and the washbasin came complete with dripping tap and exposed plumbing. Beyond it, behind a partly drawn curtain on a drooping wire, the murky recesses of what he took to be the kitchen. It was a professional reconstruction; no detail had been omitted, not even the sour mingled smell of sweat, urine and boiled cabbage.

And it was hot. Queghan hadn't realized till now but the temperature must have been in the nineties. He took his jacket off and draped it over the bedpost. Already his shirt was damp under the arms.

Blanche yelled, "That's right, go ahead, mess the place up! Whad'ya think I bin doin' all day, sitting on my butt? No respect, no consideration, I might as well be dead." She trudged across the room, scooped up the jacket, wadded it into a bundle and flung it in the corner behind the wardrobe.

"That jacket cost me—"

"Aw shaddap!" Blanche said. "You big dumb ox." She turned and faced him, hands on hips. "I ain't bin out of this dump in three days. Three days! Stuck here while you bin whorin' all over town with some cute little trick you picked up out of the gutter. Whad'ya expect me to do? Plant a big fat welcoming kiss on your ugly mug? No chance, buddy boy. You can sit there till hell freezes over, see if I care."

She turned away with a contemptuous twitch of her hips and went back to her favourite position by the window. The flickering neon sign lit her effectively, a good atmospheric prop. From the street rose the monotonous moan of a police siren.

Blanche had picked up a small ragged teddy-bear from amongst the clutter on the dresser and she cradled it to her bosom. Her voice became wistful. "We went wrong somewhere, I guess. I don't know how or why, we just did."

Queghan didn't say anything.

"No, don't say anything," Blanche said, raising her hand. "I guess it was my fault as much as yours. I wanted too much. I wanted the world and you couldn't give it to me. I guess we all gotta learn sooner or later that we can't have what we want out of life." She clutched the teddy-bear tighter. "There's a whole big world out there, you know?" she crooned softly, looking beyond the neon sign into the night sky. "When I was a kid I wanted it all, I had a right to it.

Nothin' and nobody was ever gonna stop me. But now. . ."

She glanced down at the teddy-bear nestling close to her breast. "This little fellow's only got one eye. What do you see with your one good eye, little friend? Is it still a big world out there? Can you see it all with your one good glass eye?"

"Blanche—" Queghan said.

"Don't say it. Don't make it any worse than it has to be. We both of us tried to make it work, we did our best. But sometimes I guess the odds are just a little too high." There was a choking sob in her voice.

From above came a sudden crash of breaking crockery followed by a scream, a thud, and silence.

"Whad'ya make of this crazy world, my little one-eyed friend?" asked Blanche, rocking to and fro, her voice barely audible. "With your one glass eye do you see the wickedness, the hopelessness, the broken promises, the shattered dreams? Maybe you only see the half of it. That's right, you see one side, the better side. No sense a little fellow like you taking in the whole big bad world, is there now? You see the bright side of things, the glittery success and the parties and the swell folk doin' just as it pleases them to do. Well let me tell you that your good friend Blanche here ain't never had a taste—not so much as a *sniff*—of that golden side. No sir. Blanche has bin down here all the time with the nigras and the goddam Polacks. That, I swear, is the ab-so-lute truth.

"But I have dreamed dreams. Oh dreams so high and fancy I couldn't tell you about without blushing. I do still blush, you know, though nobody in this here household would ever credit the fact. But I do. Blushin' comes easy to my fair skin. I do have a fair skin, don't I? You can see that, can't you, even with your one good glass eye?" She held the bear up in front of her, stretching out both arms. "Now isn't that just like me? How rude of me. I never did ask how come you only got just the one eye. And for that I do apologize. Might I ask? Would it embarrass you? I'm askin' as a friend, not as some pryin' intruder. If you don't wanna tell, just say so, come right out with it, I won't be offended. Goodness me, it'll take more than that to offend lil' old Blanche here—

"What's that? You were *born* with only one eye? You never had a pair of eyes in your entire life? Well as they say, and I guess it's the truth, what you ain't had you're never gonna miss. Two eyes ain't such a good thing anyway, you can take my word." She said in a harsh whisper, "With two eyes you see *everything*. Every goddam thing. And some of it ain't too pretty. I've seen a few things in my short young life that I wouldn't wish anybody to see, not anybody, not even my own worst enemy. So you're better off, little bear, take my word. With your one good glass eye you can see more than enough. And more than enough is plenty."

Right on cue the baby's cry sounded again, less strident this time, faint with tiredness. The neon sign made a fizzing noise, came on, went off, came on again uncertainly, bathing the room in an eerie green glow. Blanche leant against the window-frame, her hair a fluorescent halo, the curve of her neck and shoulders in black silhouette.

Queghan felt to be adrift in this green room. It was a fake (wasn't it?), an elaborate charade, an authentic historical reconstruction. The whole thing was a put-up job. He tried to sit up in the chair.

"Blanche . . ."

The neon light came on, went off, came on.

His senses were beginning to slide. Something about the light. His eyelids fluttered and the focal point of his consciousness began to recede, to become smaller.

He said more urgently, "Blanche," but she mustn't have heard him, still lost in dreams, the green neon light washing over her.

His consciousness had shrunk to a point of black: the contracting pupil in a glassy golden eye. The eye grew large, filled the world and he was falling inwards into the empty black centre, surrounded by green light that flickered and fizzed . . . coming on, going off, coming on.

Someone cried out. It was a voice repeating over and over again the name *Blanche* and Queghan became aware that his throat was hurting and there was wetness on his lips. He then thought in a moment of absolute calm and rational clarity:

The frequency of the light.

It was too late. He had realized too late. The light had affected the temporal lobe in the roof of the brain and this was the onset of an epileptic fit.

Léon Steele had stars in his eyes. He stood with his forehead pressed against the angled window, cracking his knuckles and wondering if this, at last, was love.

For the past two weeks he had been eating very little, just pecking at his food and then pushing the plate aside—not because he wasn't hungry but because he had been led to believe that love killed the appetite. The only flaw in this hypothesis was that he was ravenous at every mealtime and starving afterwards. But he pretended that he really couldn't face it, his emotions were too caught up, his sensibilities in a whirl of frustrated passion and poignant longing. Just a fleeting glance from her dark-brown eyes was enough to make the fluid in his bowels gurgle; though the cause might have been as much gastrological as neurochemical.

The evening (that night!) had been wonderful, a dream experience, but what had happened since had puzzled and upset him. It was almost as though she had never been to his apartment and they had not made love. His sly winkings and gentle smiles the day after had met with sharp admonitions to "Stop daydreaming, Léon. Keep your mind on what you're doing."

He thought: Was I so bad that she's forgotten already? Perhaps it never actually took place. What if I imagined it all, a schoolboy fantasy which seemed so real that I was confused into mistaking the wish for the act? But if that were so he could have lived the rest of his life in fantasy and wish-fulfilment and been perfectly happy.

Léon sighed and cracked another finger joint. The sound made him start guiltily. Pouline detested the habit and he had resolved to break himself of it; also he was supposed to be compiling a program for the cyberthetic system which could be used to discover any gremlins lurking in the RECONPAN facility. As far as he could see RECONPAN was operating as per specification. What Pouline expected to find wrong with the germanium circuitry he hadn't a notion. Perhaps she simply wanted to get back at mythographer Queghan; whenever he mentioned the man's name her colour rose up and she became quite snappish.

Léon went into the booth and put the headphones on. The curved tinted screens surrounded him cosily and the contoured seat and headrest adjusted automatically to his posture, which was semi-reclining. A red winking light at eye-level confirmed that RECONPAN was on-line. He said into the microphone:

"Datum point 27101944." There was a moment's pause, a subdued chatter of ticking relays, and the illuminated panel changed from SEARCH to READY.

Léon pressed the RECORD tab. Balancing the clipboard with the list of cross-references on his knee he began:

"State your geographical location on the day in question."

"*Wolfsschanze,** Rastenburg."

The voice was flat, impersonal, with a slight accent. Léon found nothing unusual in this; he believed he was conversing with a bunch of wires, a phalanx of silicon contact-breakers, a devil's brew of germanium solid-state circuitry. He ticked off an item on the list.

"State chronologically your movements and locations from the datum poi—from the day in question."

"I remained at *Wolfsschanze* until 20th November. Then to Berlin, where I stayed at the Chancellery until 10th December. From there I went to *Adlershorst** at Bad Nauheim, and from there, on 16th January, returned to the Reich Chancellery. From there—"

"One moment," Léon interrupted, ticking off the items.

There was a baleful silence.

"Did you stay in the Chancellery itself or in the bunker?"

"On the first occasion in the Chancellery; on the second

*"Wolf's Lair."
*"Eagle's Eyrie."

occasion in the Führerbunker due to the fact that the Chancellery had been bombed by the Americans during the latter half of December."

That tallies, Léon thought. Every date and location bang on the nail. Presumably it meant that the TCR circuit was functioning normally—though the dates could be accurate and yet the day by day summary of events wildly inaccurate. So was the facility functioning satisfactorily after all?

Léon tapped his fingers on the clipboard and cogitated for a moment. Although it had been explained to him more than once he had never properly understood what the mythographer was driving at. There were two conflicting series of events it seemed; very well: which was the true version and which the false? No, wait a minute—Queghan had said that neither was necessarily false—both could be true providing they were self-consistent. Now this was the part that confused him. How could two separate series of events covering the same period of time—*and which clearly contradicted each other*—both be accurate and true? Surely one of them had to give way in face of the other?

It was all to do with "probability," he had been told, which followed as a direct consequence of Heisenberg's Principle of Uncertainty. This stated that the position and momentum of a sub-atomic particle cannot be simultaneously determined with complete accuracy. Any conceivable method which determines the position must automatically alter the velocity of the particle; and if an attempt is made to accurately measure the momentum this again automatically affects the position. Thus the two values of a particle at a specific worldpoint can never be known with certainty.

But Léon was not, and didn't profess to be, a physicist. He felt more at home amidst the comparatively safe disciplines of electrochemical neurology and its associated bio-electric phenomena. He understood, for example, how RECONPAN could simulate the brain patterns of someone long dead (there had been talk of using the facility to recreate Shakespeare's brain-pan and have him write another masterpiece or two) because the technique could be quantified, the specification tabulated and the circuitry set down in blueprint. He was less used to—unwilling to accept—the nebulous uncertainties of Myth Technology and the flights of fancy to which it ascended. Like Pouline deGrenier he was a pragmatist born and bred.

The next item read: "Personnel in Führerbunker, 22nd April—1st May, 1945, inclusive."

Léon fed the datum point into the facility and when the panel changed from SEARCH to READY yawningly put forward his query. Back came the methodical answer:

"Reichsjugendführer Arthur Axmann, Rittmeister Gerhard Friedrich Boldt, Chef Lufwaffenführungsstab Eckard Christian, Frau Gerda Christian, Reich Chancellor Joseph Goebbels, Frau Goebbels, Wehrmachtattaché Major Willi Johannmeier, Frau Gertraud Junge, Revieroberwachtmeister Hermann Karnau, General Feldmarschall Wilhelm Keitel, SS Sturmbannführer Erich Kempka, Fräulein Else Krueger, Heinz Lorenz, Baron Major Freytag von Loringhoven, SS Hauptscharführer Erich Mansfeld, Dr. Theodor Morell, Otto Willi Mueller, Heinz Matthiesing, Hilco Poppen, Flugkapitän Hanna Reitsch, SS Hauptsturmführer Guenther Schwaegermann, Baroness von Varo."

Down the page a row of neat red ticks. Pouline would be pleased at this. She was fanatical so far as RECONPAN was concerned; indeed he wondered what else in life motivated her or brought a sparkle to her eye.

"Certainly not sex," he said aloud. "She couldn't be less interested." He bethought himself. "Unless it's just me she's not interested in."

"You have problems of that kind too?" said the simulated brain of the Führer, a response generated from the electrically-charged tissue cultures and transmitted at 350 feet per second along the branches of the axon fibre, passed electrochemically through the synapse, converted from charged sodium and potassium atoms into differential wave patterns and thence via the germanium circuit to the headphones.

"Yes," said Léon morosely. "One minute she leads me on and the next she doesn't want to know. It's been the same all my life. I suppose women don't find me attractive."

"Is there something the matter with you? Physically?"

"I don't think so," Léon said, trying to give an honest answer. "I'm not handsome, I know. I'm not the kind of man women dream about; but looks aren't everything, are they?" He made himself more comfortable in the contoured chair. "To be truthful, women have always disappointed me. Even the intelligent ones like Pouline seem to be taken in by surface show. Do you know what I mean? You'd think they'd see through all that to the person underneath, the real person. I have a very loving nature, my mother always said so, but women don't seem to find that important. Oh they *say* it's important, they say they prefer a man to be gentle and considerate and understanding but they always go for the other kind, the selfish bigoted louts who treat them like dirt. I find that very confusing."

"I only ever loved once—the one woman."

"All your life?"

"Yes."

"That would be Fräulein Braun."

There was a perceptible, a significant, pause.

"Frau Hitler."

"Ah yes. Yes of course." Léon nodded, his eyes caught and held by the winking red light. It seemed to be a time for meditative reflection, for confession even. He wished he smoked a pipe, it would have completed the image. Red lights—two of them—were glassily reflected in his wide dreamy eyes.

He said, "The trouble is, between you and me, I don't like women. I mean I fancy them sexually, I'd like to sleep with the attractive ones—I'm not ambiguous in that sense—but I don't really like them. I feel uncomfortable in their company. It's as if I can only think of them in one way, as sexual objects, and they seem to sense this and it frightens them off. It's only with ugly women that I can talk easily and because they're ugly I've no interest in them. I can talk to Karla

Ritblat but that's only because she's old and I don't think of her in a sexual way at all."

"Ritblat," said the voice of the brain in his ear. "Is she by any chance Jewish?"

"Not sure," Léon said vaguely. "Could be, I suppose. She prepared the tissue cultures."

"Explain to me."

"The living tissue which provides the interaction between the data-processing function in the cerebrum and the generation of conscious thought. They allow you to think."

"They allow me to think?"

"Yes."

"And Ritblat prepared these tissue cultures?"

"Yes."

"*Urglhhmaaach!*"

It was a sound approximating to the slow and infinitely painful strangulation of a small furry animal by barbed wire.

"I wish you wouldn't do that," Léon said, irritated. "It gives me a headache."

"What do you suppose it does to me?" asked the brain of the Führer. "I have memories."

"Haven't we all?" Léon sighed.

"Your memories are nothing compared to mine."

"I suppose not."

"Your life is nothing compared to mine."

"I wouldn't go as far as that," Léon said, nettled. "Just because you're an historical figure, somebody who made his mark, doesn't mean to say that your life is more important than mine. Every life has its own unique significance."

"Scheisse!*"

"Pardon?"

"I said 'unquestionably.' "

"You agree?"

"I do, I do."

"Do you know?" An opinion had formed in Léon's head. "I think history misjudged you." He folded his arms and

*Crap!

gazed at the winking red light. "The record files in Archives make you out to be a raving madman but you're nothing of the sort. In fact you're a very sympathetic person. I really feel I can talk to you, confide in you. You're the kind of person, I should imagine, who was misunderstood."

"Oh I was," the brain of Hitler agreed readily. "Definitely misunderstood. History has been distorted, the truth has been suppressed and lies put in its place. Treachery and deceit and evil plots—everything which surrounded me all through my life has been allowed to pervert the true picture. I have been slandered by destiny."

"You had problems just like everyone else."

"Hundreds of problems. Insurmountable problems. Nobody knows the half of it. Except Eva and Theo."

"Theo?"

"Mein Leibarzt, Dr. Morell. He was one of my closest companions for many years."

Léon consulted the list. "Your personal physician. Which reminds me, we never did manage to research him thoroughly for the Subject Profile. The records were incomplete. We could only feed in the barest details of his life."

"He was a strange man," the brain said. "Secretive. He kept a diary, I believe, though no one ever saw it. His theories on the vital forces at work within the human body were fascinating. Pity about the diary, it would have made interesting reading."

"It should be on file somewhere," Léon said, making a note. "I'll have a look for it in Archives."

"Tell me," said the brain of the Führer, a note of casual inquiry in the bland emotionless voice.

"Yes?"

"Is this Ritblat person to be trusted? You say she developed the tissue cultures which provide me with conscious thought. There is no doubt as to her . . . loyalty?"

"Karla Ritblat is a dedicated and experienced psychomedical research scientist. Are you questioning her professional integrity?"

"You have no doubts at all?"

"None. Why do you ask?"

The relays hummed, the red light winked. Léon listened intently to the soft simulated voice in the headphones.

"I wouldn't like to think that somebody of an inferior race has been tampering with the dynamic metabolism of my brain. Do not forget that I am the greatest military strategist of all time!"

Blanche came away from the window, saying, "Shaddap, ya drunken bum." She stood by his chair.

"Oh my sweet Christ," she said, falling to her knees.

Queghan was unconscious, his eyeballs upturned into his head, saliva running freely down his chin. He was slowly choking to death with his tongue. Blanche was transfixed. In her terror and numbed panic she tore one of the arms off the teddy bear. The big dumb Polack was going to die. Right here in front of her eyes.

His limbs were rigid, the legs sticking out like wooden stilts. The neon light gave his face the appearance of a greenish death mask. His eyes were blank staring white.

She thought, I can't let him die, he's my husband . . . and then, You stupid bloody fool, the Dilantin.

For a frozen eternity of time she couldn't remember how to get out of the apartment. Two of the doors were false, leading nowhere, and her mind refused to make a decision. When she finally moved it was with the agonizing slowness of a dream; things got in her way and hindered her and she saw her own snail-like progress from above, her mind distanced from the inept fumbling body below trying to open doors and stumbling headlong into objects. This detached part of her mind thought, If he dies because of my childish daydreams . . .

The syringe in the vinyl pouch was ready-charged. She extracted it carefully from the sheath, rolled up his sleeve and injected the full amount directly into the vein. His face was the colour of chalk and running with perspiration.

What next, what next, what next? She couldn't think. He had told her, very exactly, what had to be done. Now she remembered, and reaching into his mouth uncurled his tongue, with the other hand tearing the hem off her dress and folding it into a pad and, still holding his mouth apart, pushed the wad of material between his teeth.

What if he dies? Oria thought, kneeling helplessly by the side of the chair. *What if he dies?*

8

The Anti-Matter Man

The CENTiNEL findings came through sooner than anyone expected, and Johann Karve was no exception. He had allowed Professor Herff and his team several weeks at the least, possibly months, before any results were obtained which could be construed as significant. Herein lay another moot point: on whose interpretation did this significance depend? Herff was in charge of the Particle Accelerator and had an established reputation as an astrophysicist but he was not familiar with the finer points of Myth Technology. It was actually up to Karve to study them, ponder their significance, and extrapolate from them meaningful conclusions.

The sheer volume of statistical data was daunting. The profusion of sub-atomic interactions at temperatures in the region of one thousand billion degrees was, to the theoreticians, somewhat embarrassing. There were charmed quarks, red quarks, black quarks, heavy leptons, neutrinos, mu-mesons, and in most instances their anti-matter companions whose life-spans were longer than the rule-book allowed by several millionths of a second.

Most disturbing of all—and yet equally intriguing—was the unmistakeable presence of Hadrons, the genus of matter associated with the creation of the universe in the first micro-second after its birth. In an appendix to the report Herff had stressed that the preponderance of Hadrons in that particular spatio-temporal co-ordinate might be due to the proximity of *2U0525-06* whose time dilation interference would have an effect on the structure and behaviour of sub-atomic particles. In other words the Black Hole, in slowing time and light to a dead stop, made a mockery of earthbound physics and the premises on which scientists based their hypotheses.

Herff had written: "There is no disputing that Hadrons are here in force. I draw no conclusions from this fact, I simply state it. Perhaps you and mythographer Queghan might care to speculate on the whys and wherefores and the probable consequences."

Was there a flippant irony between the lines? In his lonely outpost on the *Tempus* satellite it would be understandable if Max had a jaundiced view of the *prima donnas* back on Earth IVn who whiled away the hours chasing exotic multi-coloured butterflies in cloud-cuckoo-land. And yet, and yet . . . the explanation was here if only he had the wit to find it; with Queghan out of the running it looked as though the task had settled squarely on his ageing shoulders.

Karve pressed the intercom tab and asked for a pot of tea. A feeling of bleak desolation descended upon him: I have to begin all over again, he thought, and there is no one to help me. Does it never end? Do we just go on and on, solving one problem only to be faced by ten more? Yet why should this depress me when my entire life has been dedicated to this singular purpose? We shall never answer all the questions because the ultimate question will always remain: What Next?

As a young man Johann Karve had sought to reconcile the four prime energy sources with the psychic processes which manifested themselves through the human mind. A complementary sphere of scientific inquiry—MetaPsychical Research—had to a large extent taken over this work, its objective being to integrate all psi phenomena and neurochemical data into the one cohesive structure. Thereafter Karve had concerned himself more with symbolism and mythology as concentrated expressions of the roots of human psyche. His inspiration in those early days had been Carl

Gustav Jung, the Swiss psychiatrist who in the early-Twentieth Pre-Colonization had laid the foundation for what was to become, many centuries later, the metaphysical science known as Myth Technology. Jung, in fact, had been the first "Myth Technologist," seeking to interpret signs and omens in terms relevant to the wellsprings of psychic energy (the "libido" to use the Jungian term).

The very real basis of the science was contained in Jung's writings: "Symbols are never devised consciously but are always produced out of the unconscious by way of revelation or intuition." In the same way dream-images, visions, extrasensory perception and myths were the concentrated manifestations of subjective experience. As he wrote elsewhere: "We are forced to view the world as a psychic phenomenon. Certainly it is necessary for science to know how things are 'in themselves,' but even science cannot escape the psychological conditions of knowledge."

Distant as it may have seemed at first glance it was only a short step from this study of the dynamics of the psyche to the theories advanced by the relativitists and quantum physicists—for they too were dealing in the statistical probabilities of reality as opposed to hard-and-fast criteria in a mechanistic universe.

"The philosophical principle that underlies our conception of natural law is *causality,*" Jung wrote. "But if the connection between cause and effect turns out to be only statistically valid and only relatively true, then the causal principle is only of relative use for explaining natural processes and therefore presupposes the existence of one or more other factors which would be necessary for an explanation. This is as much to say that the connection of events may in certain circumstances be other than causal, and requires another principle of explanation . . ."

So there, thought Karve, was a possible solution if one was prepared to accept it. Not that the acausal nature of spacetime was a new or original concept; mathematical evidence supported by laboratory experiment had provided the phenomenon with a respectable pedigree—notably the Ernst-Ryan-Gathorne Experiment*—and it was now taught as a supplementary subject to students of high-energy particle physics.

But was he going to be so intellectually outlandish as to suggest that Hadrons from 14 billion years ago were meddling with casuality and creating "psi world"—mythical planes of existence on which alternative scenarios were taking place? The two questions which immediately presented themselves were How and Why?

How could a species of ultra-sub-atomic particles interfere in a squalid and rather obscure war which had taken place hundreds of years Pre-Colonization? Was it perhaps a simulation exercise in which anti-Hadrons assumed the infrastructure of a period and followed the events through to their logical (or in this instance, illogical) conclusion? A kind of historical reconstruction on a cosmic scale?

If the How was baffling, the Why was doubly so. Assuming that the Hadrons were a form of subnuclear intelligence roaming at will through the universe, what possible motive could they have for creating a mythical landscape? Perhaps they were unaware of the havoc they were causing in this stratum of spacetime, knew nothing and cared even less about disrupting the decay rates of particles which comprised Karve's universe. There was no reason to regard them as possessing evil intent. They were intelligent, and being intelligent presumably had moral and ethical codes of behaviour; but just as a man will crush minute organisms by walking on them, totally blameless, not wishing them harm, so the Hadrons could trample unthinkingly on an organism they only dimly perceived, if at all.

"They could be here now, in this room," Karve murmured. "And neither of us is aware of the presence of the other."

Two alien life-forms moving through each other, one in time, the other in minus time, just occasionally the two

*See Appendix: *Causality*.

indistinct edges of their spacetime continuums meeting at the matter/anti-matter interface.

The tea in the pot, when he remembered to pour it, was lukewarm. He drank it unsweetened, with a slice of lemon, and contemplated the material piled on the desk in front of him.

The First Assistant apologized for disturbing him but said that Queghan's wife was in the outer office; could he spare the time to see her? She was pale, composed, and sat down immediately in the chair, frowning at the carpet. He offered her some tea but she didn't respond.

"Have you seen him, Johann?"

Karve saw that she wore no make-up and that her blond hair was brushed severely back from the face, catching a reflected sheen of light from the window. He put the cup and saucer on the tray. "No, I haven't. They're keeping me informed of his progress. There's no need to worry."

"It was my fault."

"Nonsense."

"This time it was my fault," she said more firmly.

Karve made a small helpless gesture and said, "You've been married to him long enough now to know that these attacks are unavoidable. Sometimes they can be controlled and sometimes we have to let them run their course. We have all the facilities in Psycho-Med to ensure he receives the best possible attention. Karla Ritblat is expert in this field; Chris couldn't be in better hands."

"I don't doubt her ability," Oria said, gazing at the floor. "But I nearly let him die. He was having an attack and I just used it as part of my fantasy. He could have been lying dead in the chair and I'd have gone on acting out my silly dreamscapes."

"That didn't happen."

"It could have."

"But it didn't." Karve looked at her steadily. "We can't concern ourselves with what might have been, only with what is," yet even as he said this he realized with mocking self-deprecation that he spent his entire professional life concerning himself with statistical probabilities—the might-have-been as distinct from actual everyday reality. In some probable alternative scenario Queghan could have died, would have done, and had.

He said, "Have you been to see him?"

"Yes, just now. He's still in coma." She made an attempt to smile. "At least I did the right thing in giving him the Dilantin. I nearly didn't find that until it was too late. What a bloody hopeless stupid broad I am. Jeez."

It seemed to Karve that she felt an obligation to break down. The real emotion was lacking, although unshed tears weren't enough to expiate her remorse. He tried to comfort her.

"Chris is going to be all right. Within a week, ten days, he'll be back on his feet. Karla told me herself that there's no cause for alarm. Oria, I promise you that he'll pull through. Chris is a tough customer to get rid of."

"But with my help he'll manage it."

"Don't be stupid, you love him, you don't wish him harm—"

"Why don't you tell me that I'm just upset and I'll get over it? I'm good at that scene, word perfect. I'll even cry if you want. Tears to order, on request."

"If you want me to absolve you from guilt I can't do it," Karve said gently. "And if you want to take the entire blame for a physiological condition he was born with, go ahead. But we both know that whatever you do he'll still have these attacks from time to time. Chris is a mythographer; he is not as other men are."

Oria was silent for a while. She looked into his eyes. "Is it true that you spoke to Karla and that she said—?"

"*Yes.*" Karve smiled at her. "Do you think I'd be sitting here drinking cold tea if I didn't know he was going to be all right?"

Oria shook her head quickly, an abrupt giddy movement like that of a little girl. "I have to dramatize everything. I can't live life without creating scenes." She faltered. "If Chris died I wouldn't have anything to live for. You see,

Johann, I don't believe in anything, least of all myself. Chris is my hold on reality and if he wasn't here I'd go mad."

Karve was left with nothing to say, this time lost for facile words.

Pouline deGrenier sat alone in the darkened office. Through the curved panel to her left she could see the flickering display of lights in the laboratory: symmetrical patterns of red, green, orange and magenta glowing momentarily in sequence and then going out, glowing, going out as in some mysterious and inexplicable ritual. Now and then came the faint whirr of a timing device followed by the subdued *click* of a circuit-breaker disconnecting itself according to predetermined plan.

The laboratory ticked and hummed to itself with an oleaginous self-satisfied smugness that of late had begun to unnerve her. She thought, I created all this and yet it frightens me. Is there something here, something unknown which I sense yet cannot comprehend? Or is the fear inside me, a projection of my own doubts and neuroses? I'm actually here inside the brain of someone long dead, she thought. All around me a billion neurological impulses are scurrying back and forth with bits of information, like mice carrying tiny pieces of cheese.

And as always, when alone in the laboratory late at night, she experienced the slow rising surge of sexual heat attempting to overpower her senses.

It was an actual taste in her mouth, a thick glutinous taste and a heavy dense odour which made her knees tremble and turned her backbone to water. Did the brain wish to make love to her? Did it want to enter into her as she, at this moment, was inside it, aware of its cerebral processes scampering all around?

Suddenly she giggled. The sound was abruptly loud and shocked her by its high-pitched edge of hysteria. She thought that she was about to lose control and break out in maniacal shrieks of laughter. What was happening to her? It was as if she was on a mountain-top and the handrails which kept her securely in place had been removed and the drop loomed before her, slippery-steep, with nothing to clutch at and stop her sliding over except thin rarefied air.

This is madness, she thought, and the word in her mind made her sweat coldly. It was overwork, nervous strain, the combined effect of the two—a dozen reasons to explain it away. The project had demanded too much of her time, that was it; bound to be psychologically unhealthy, she told herself with prim firmness.

Pouline looked through the transparent panel into the laboratory and somebody or something was obscuring the lights. It was an outline, marked by winking patterns of red, green, orange, magenta—

She stopped breathing. Was it him? Had he materialized from the machine, risen like an evil wraith from the germanium circuitry and was now made flesh, bone, brain and spirit, standing out there in the flickering laboratory? It wasn't possible, she was hallucinating, he wasn't really there, only in her mind, and as she thought this the shadow moved across the lights and came towards the door of the office.

It was some time later that she discovered she had drawn blood from the palms of her hands, the pressure of her fists forcing the nails into the flesh. The actual moment when he entered the office was a frozen splinter of eternity, and even when the light revealed his face and she saw who it was her blank disbelief held her in a state of suspension; then the air flooded from her lungs and her body relaxed.

His face, Pouline noticed, seemed oddly luminous in the dim light: translucent almost.

"I didn't expect anyone to be there, least of all you." A sudden rush of blood made her cheeks glow with heat.

"You have a morbid fascination for sitting alone in the dark."

"Is it morbid? I don't see why."

"The spirits might haunt you."

"I don't believe in such things."

He went to the panel and looked through into the laboratory. Without turning his head he said, "I wish I could be that certain."

"Certain of what?"

"Anything at all."

Pouline laughed nervously. "I was under the impression that Myth Technologists knew all the answers."

"It isn't the task of the Myth Technologist to provide the answers; only to ask the questions."

"How modest of you."

"Not me," Queghan said, turning. "That was a quote from Johann Karve's manual for fledgling mythographers, *The Hidden Universe*."

"I thought mythographers were born, not made."

"Yes indeed. But we need guidance. We need to be taught how to use our gift."

"Is it a gift?" Pouline asked curiously. And then, "I'm not even sure what it is you're able to do. It's never been properly explained to me."

"Didn't I explain it to you?"

"When?"

She watched his face, holding her breath.

"Have you forgotten?"

"I don't know." She was confused. A misplaced memory nagged at her. "When?"

"That night."

Pouline stared at him.

"You have forgotten."

"I'm not sure; but you seem to remember it."

"I do indeed."

"That's the second time you've used the word 'indeed.' "

"Now you're thinking like a mythographer."

"I don't understand."

"Picking up unconsidered trifles and trying to make something of them."

"Is that what mythographers do?" she asked gravely, a

small puzzled frown on her face.

"Part of it. We're not interested in the set-pieces of life, only in the margins, the things that in the jargon 'aggregate by mutual indifference.' "

"You mean there's no connection between them?"

"No causal connection," Queghan amended.

He sat down in the chair across the desk from her. Pouline thought it strange that although his face was in darkness she could see every feature clearly delineated, as though illuminated from within. He said:

"The fatal thing is to concentrate on the events; rather we ignore them and gradually they form into an acausal pattern which we can detect and interpret."

"Can anyone detect them?"

"They can and do, though most people brush them aside as 'just another coincidence.' They don't see any special significance in an apparently unrelated sequence of events—but that's because they're looking for a causal connection which fits in with their everyday experience. Mythic events, by their very nature, don't obey the rules we impose on objective reality. If I were to tell you that the reason you have brown eyes is due to the fact that Léon Steele finds them attractive you'd find it difficult to accept."

"Impossible," Pouline deGrenier said. "The fact of my having brown eyes precedes the fact of Léon Steele finding them attractive by some thirty years."

"What has time to do with it? We're dealing with acausality, not horology. You're thinking of events in terms of everyday experience: it's quite feasible that something might happen tomorrow which affects your behaviour last week."

He was smiling at her so that Pouline felt like a child having something simple explained to it which it failed to grasp, and even as she was thinking this a light seemed to go on in a dim dusty corner of her mind. She said, "That's why you set such great store by probability . . . you never state definitely that an event has or will take place, only the probable likelihood of it taking place—"

"And the most important concept of all," Queghan said

softly, "is that the incidence of probability can never be resolved. It is, by definition, an unknown and unknowable quantity, for ever in a state of uncertainty. Everything in the universe, from a sub-atomic particle upwards, exists within a certain tolerance, a vague shadowy area which marks the boundary of knowledge. It is the limit to what we can ever know."

"Everything?"

"Every single thing. Events at the subnuclear level or on a cosmological scale. Spacetime, history, the past, the future, even relationships between people. Morality, ethics, the whole bag of tricks."

"Everything is constantly relative," Pouline said.

"Or relatively constant."

"And ultimately unknowable."

"With absolute Godlike certainty, yes."

It might have been an omen, a presentiment—for Pouline deGrenier suddenly experienced a keen and disturbing sense of *déjà vu*. She had lived through this before. This conversation had already taken place in some distant past—a dreamscape shrouded in ambiguity like the images in a distorting mirror. One of the images steadied and sharpened: the form and likeness of Léon Steele, and Pouline thought, Not with him. I couldn't. I didn't . . .

She could remember approaching the desk, this desk, and picking up the receiver and selecting the code . . . and then the image shivered and it was as though there were two Pouline deGreniers going their separate ways, two people in different shifting worlds which seemed to overlap like a series of transparent overlays one on top of the other.

Could I have been in two places at once? she wondered. And if Léon was one of my lovers, who was the other?

"We can never know anything for certain," Queghan said. "The ultimate mystery remains."

"I now understand why Myth Technology is regarded as a metaphysical science." She looked across the desk at Queghan and knew, without any doubt whatsoever, that just below his left collar-bone there was a mark. She had traced its imprint with the tips of her fingers: a shallow pale indentation in the shape of a Q. But how was this possible?

"It is strange, isn't it?"

"What?" she said, her heart lurching in her chest.

"What you are thinking."

Fear made her voice cold and impersonal. "Do you know what I'm thinking?"

His hand went up to his left shoulder and he tapped the spot with his long delicate fingers. She could see through them: they were translucent: she could see the shapes of the bones inside.

"What's happening?" she said aghast. "What's wrong with you?"

When Queghan smiled she could see the skull underneath.

"Mythographers do more than interpret the meaning of coincidences and wait for events to aggregate by mutual indifference. We are blessed—some might say cursed—with the gift of mythic projection."

"I don't know what—"

"I think you do."

"No!" she said, refusing to listen, to accept. But she did know what he meant, the knowledge was full-born in her mind. It was a revelation, precise in every detail. "Is this a dream?" she asked. "Is it really happening?"

"Do you believe it's happening?" Inside his skull she could see the shadowy bulky mass of the brain. The living brain inside the skull.

The palms of her hands were sticky with sweat and blood. "If it is really happening I must be going mad, and if it isn't I must be mad already."

Queghan raised his hand, a hand that had the substance of gossamer, to indicate the room in which they sat. "Look around you."

Pouline turned and saw blank grey walls of concrete, shiny with condensation. The low ceiling was a solid slab of masonry with a caged bulb in the centre and the desk in front of her was a rough wooden table with papers scattered over it. There were no windows and just a single metal door painted green, the rivets protruding sufficiently to throw elongated shadows down to the floor. The floor too was concrete, gritty underfoot, and she could smell the chill decaying dampness of an underground tomb. There was no sound except her own breathing, the uneven flutter of air in her nostrils and the internal sounds inside her eardrums as the blood swished and gurgled through her body.

"What is this place?" she asked in a whisper.

"I think we should have to call it . . ." he was practically transparent now ". . . a region of probability."

Yet it was real to her, it was too real. Pouline could feel the damp and cold entering into her pores. And the odour of stale air and decay and sweating concrete filled her mouth and nose. There was evil here too, palpable and overpowering. She shivered involuntarily and closed her eyes. This was what he had meant by mythic projection—the ability to place an image inside her head and force her to see and feel and smell its reality. Did it exist? And where was it? Was she actually and literally here, enclosed within concrete walls and slabs of masonry?

"Am I really here?" she asked him. "Am I?"

There was a sharp cracking sound close to her left ear and Pouline opened her eyes to see Lón Steele standing anxiously over her, pulling at his fingers. He stopped guiltily when her eyes focused on him.

"Are you all right? Can I get you something?"

"Where's Queghan?"

Léon glanced round the office. "I don't know. Is he here?"

Of course he wasn't: the chair was empty.

9

In the Führerbunker

Berlin, April 1945
These are dark days. As Schwerin von Krosigk remarked to me only yesterday: "All this week there has been nothing but a succession of Job's messengers. How will it end? How *can* it end?"

Living down here, hidden away from the daylight and fresh air, it is indeed difficult to gain a true perspective on what is happening throughout the country. All the reports are bad. We hear that the Americans are over the Elbe and that the Russians have crossed the Oder and are marching on Dresden and threatening Berlin itself. In the north a combined force of Japanese and Americans are meeting little resistance as they approach Bremen and Hamburg, and in the south the French are swarming along the upper Danube, having already taken Vienna. Even the Führer's sacred Bavaria is threatened by General Patton and his merciless armoured brigades.

But the worst news of all came this morning. Goebbels sent a personal messenger from his headquarters in the cellars beneath the Propaganda Ministry with an urgent dispatch which dealt a blow to the heart: the Blackshirts have capitulated. Our hopes had all been pinned on their holding the Low Countries and opening a corridor through to Berlin as a means of escape, but now we hear that Montgomery has entered into negotiations with Eisenhower in the hope of saving the remnants of the 7th Army. As a final cruel sting in the tail the message added that the Leibstandarte AH, the Führer's personal SS Division, had been a party to the surrender and is now no more.

The conditions down here, twenty metres below ground underneath the Chancellery, leave a lot to be desired. Our quarters are perpetually damp and even the air-conditioning cannot get rid of the smell of many human beings forced to live like animals on top of one another, day in and day out. The Führerbunker consists of eighteen rooms (little more than concrete cubicles) divided by a central passageway which is used as a general sitting area and, further along behind a wooden partition, a space where the daily staff conferences are held. On either side of this narrow passage are the private rooms: on the left Hitler's bedroom and study, and next to these Eva's bedroom, bathroom and dressing-room. A small ante-room adjoining these is used by the Führer's personal SS bodyguard.

My two rooms—bedroom and office—along with Stumpfegger's bedroom and first-aid station are on the right of the passage; further along are the rooms which contain the emergency telephone exchange, the guardroom and the Diesel power house. At our end of the Bunker we are fortunate in having the emergency exit which leads up four flights of concrete stairs to the Chancellery garden. But even the close proximity of this isn't much of a comfort, for there is a general standing order that no one is allowed outside until after dark and then only for a maximum period of forty-five minutes. It's like living in a submarine moored permanently at the bottom of the Arctic Ocean. Cold, damp, depressing.

Every day there is a constant stream of visitors: Doenitz, Bormann, Keitel, Jodl, Kesselring, Christian, Speer, Krebs, and dozens of aides and adjutants ferrying messages back and forth. I try, as much as possible, not to get too involved in the continuous and wearying round of staff meetings, map conferences, Orders to General Staff, and so on. I find it very tedious and there isn't much to be gleaned by listening to their endless inane chatter, so I stay in my room writing my diary and reading Carlyle's *History of Frederick the Great* (the

Führer's personal copy, which I borrowed). Sometimes I while away the hours by chatting(!) to Eva in the comparative privacy of her bedroom. We are rarely disturbed there, which is convenient.

Much of the current activity, I gather, is concerned with persuading the Führer to move south to Obersalzberg. Bormann puts in an appearance several times a day, emerging from the SS Bunker under the Party Chancellery and making a dash (brave soul!) to be by the Führer's side, imploring him to move his headquarters before the Russians encircle the city. His pleadings are backed by Himmler, Goebbels and Krebs, and all four are passionate in their entreaties to withdraw south while the opportunity remains. But the Führer is unmoved. He listens to their pleas, slumped in his chair, his face ashen, and when they have finished launches into his battle plans for the week ahead; it's as though they haven't spoken—indeed I'd be very surprised if he hears a single word they say.

After one of these abortive "conferences," which go on for three hours or more, Goebbels took me to one side and told me in the strictest confidence that he was concerned for the Führer's sanity. He didn't actually mention that word but instead spoke delicately of "his mental condition." Was there nothing to be done? he wanted to know. Couldn't I prescribe something which would restore his mental faculties to their usual peak of sustained intellectual brilliance?

I answered that I was apportioning the remaining supply of drugs on a very careful rota to ensure they would last out till fresh supplies arrived. "When these are gone," I said sombrely, "he will not live three days. You have my word as an experienced medical practitioner."

"Thank God you are still loyal, Theo," Goebbels said fervently. "There are some close to the Führer I view with the greatest suspicion. Though it may not be apparent, both Goering and Himmler are panic-stricken, out of their wits with fear. It will not be long before the rats desert the sinking ship."

His dark intelligent eyes and lean sallow face were grave in aspect and he was himself obviously in the depths of depression.

"I have never let you down, Herr Reichsminister," I said to him fiercely, "and I do not intend to start now."

He patted my shoulder and there was a glint of life in his eyes. "Good man. As long as we remain faithful to the Führer there is hope yet that we shall conquer all. The Reich will triumph. His will be done!"

A touching little scene in the Chancellery garden during the afternoon. Reichsjugendführer Axmann, leader of the Hitler Youth Movement, brought a squad of boys along to receive the Führer's blessing. These are the last-ditch defence troops about to be sent into action against the Russian onslaught which every day advances ten kilometres towards Berlin.

Grasping the opportunity for a little sunshine and fresh air additional to our quota, Eva and I stood near the concrete observation tower and watched as the Führer hobbled along the line of boys, most of them not more than fourteen years old, shaking their hands, patting their unblemished cheeks, and pinning medals to their warriors' chests. They stood proudly, conscious of the historical immensity of the occasion, and made a beautiful picture for the film camera which Goebbels, always ready to use every conceivable situation for propaganda purposes, had arranged for with his usual unobtrusive efficiency.

I am almost prepared to swear that the Führer had tears in his eyes as he reached the end of the line. He looked up from his stooping crouch and seemed to turn away abruptly as if overcome by the unflinching patriotism in those young faces of the future, faces unlined by five years of war or any of life's tribulations and harrowing disappointments. It was a glorious moment and one I shall always treasure.

Due to the events of the day, that same evening in the Führerbunker was one of melancholy reflection and nostalgia for the bright dead days of long ago. There were several of us gathered together, sitting on hard straight chairs in the anteroom to the Führer's quarters, listening to the non-stop monologue which is his mode of conversation whenever he's had a little too much wine and is in a contemplative frame of mind. It went on for some considerable time and I must confess I dozed off once or twice, so my recollection of what was said is sketchy and incomplete. However the gist of it was to the effect that he had missed his true path in life, taken the wrong direction, regretted his mistakes, etc, etc.

One of the adjutants present (I think it was Rittmeister Boldt) asked what on earth the Führer could mean by such a declaration, obviously playing the part of the slimy fawning toad for the evening. Hitler replied that he was not, never had been and what's more had no ambition to be, a politician. "Many people have commented on the fact—probably you yourself have noticed it—that I have an artistic nature."

"Certainly, certainly," Boldt assented at once, nodding his stupid empty head like a mechanical doll's.

"I appreciate the finer things of life, the aesthetic virtues. I should, by rights, have been an artist. My nature rebels against regimentation, something that should be obvious to anyone with eyes in his head."

We all nodded at how obvious this obviously was.

He went on, "But I was persuaded to thwart my artistic inclinations and instead to lead the German people along the road of National Socialism in order that they might fulfil their historic destiny. It is untrue that I, or anybody else in Germany, wanted war in 1939. It was wanted and provoked exclusively by those international politicians who either came of Jewish stock or worked for Jewish interests. After all my offers of disarmament, posterity cannot place the responsibility for this war on me. My true nature was violated and I was forced, against my better judgement, to become Führer of the Fatherland. What couldn't I have been? What couldn't I have achieved as an architect, say, or a painter of landscapes? All gone, wasted, my talents cast aside and not allowed to flower."

"Some seeds fall on stony ground," a voice murmured, possibly under the mistaken impression that this was apposite to the Führer's melancholic meanderings.

Fortunately Hitler was listening only to the sound of his own voice and he rambled on in this vein for the next twenty minutes. Finally he took it into his head to send one of the secretaries for his horoscope, the one drawn up on 30th January, 1933, and we spent the next hour perusing this sacred document in the hope that it might point to a way out of the present difficulties.

The predictions (I must admit) were shattering. It forecast that war would break out in 1939, that the Allies would win victory after victory until the summer of '42, and then would follow a series of defeats until, in the autumn of 1944, the tide would turn against us and the Reich would be subject to tremendous pressure. In the spring of 1945, stalemate—and then in May a new and unexpected factor would suddenly emerge to change the course of the war. Further inactivity would follow till August, and finally peace. The three years after this would be a difficult time for Germany but from 1948 onwards it would rise to its former greatness.

Otto Guensche, Hitler's SS adjutant, was the first to voice the puzzlement that many in the room felt. He sat by the Führer's right elbow, a large heavily-built man with a vee of wrinkles descending from a receding hairline, and inquired what this "new and unexpected factor" could be. Everyone waited in a hush of expectancy.

"What can it mean?" the Führer said, looking round the circle of curious faces. "It can mean only one thing: the wonder weapon."

I saw the light of hope and enthusiasm die in the eyes of those gathered in the small cramped smelly room, for we all knew that insurmountable technical problems had forestalled the development of the so-called "Atomic Bomb" and many of us had long since lost all faith in it as a credible means of saving the Reich, even were it to be used as a propaganda threat. All through 1944 we had been waiting with growing impatience for the announcement that it was ready to be tested; the rumour had it that the Bomb would be detonated in Yugoslavia or Bulgaria, wiping out a major city or two as a demonstration and a warning of its awesome effect. Nothing had come of this grandiose scheme and the Bomb was nowadays rarely mentioned, and even then as a sour joke. The fact that the Führer still believed it to be a decisive factor in winning the war for the Allies only gave rise to greater fears as to his—to use Goebbels' euphemistic phrase—"mental condition."

It is now two days since the Führer's birthday (20th April) and the atmosphere down here in the Bunker is strained to the limit of desperation and despair. Sporadic artillery fire has been heard in the southern suburbs and our intelligence service reports that it is the Russian pincer movement tightening its grip on Berlin.

Yesterday the Führer ordered an all-out attack and took personal command of battle operations. As head of the force he placed SS Obergruppenführer Steiner, with explicit instructions to deploy every man, every tank and every aircraft in the defence of the city. The final briefing conference was tense and, on occasion, traumatic. He summoned the remnants of his senior staff, including Steiner and Karl Koller, the General der Luftwaffe, and told them that he would not accept failure, no matter what excuses they might have to offer. Towards the end he had worked himself up into a frenzy, stamping his feet on the concrete floor and screaming at them: "Any commanding officer who keeps men back will forfeit his life within five hours! You will guarantee with your heads that absolutely every man is employed!"

For twelve hours we awaited the outcome of the battle. Had the Russians been repulsed or were they making headway? The Führer sent message after message demanding confirmation that the attack had been launched but the reports were conflicting: Himmler telephoned to say that it had taken place and the enemy advance had been halted; then came a report from the Luftwaffe saying that no such encounter had taken place. Hitler was in a ferment, grey-faced, shaking, eyes blood-shot with rage and fatigue, and I was twice called upon during the afternoon to administer additional injections to regulate his pulse and blood-pressure. He was becoming less and less aware of his surroundings, staring through people as though they didn't exist.

At four o'clock in the afternoon a special conference was called, with Bormann, Burgdorf, Keitel, Jodl and Krebs attending. It turned out to be an exhausting marathon which went on till the early hours of the next day. Nothing, it appears, had been done: General Steiner hadn't ordered the attack: the battle was a mythical one, existing only in the Führer's brain.

Then he went berserk.

Screaming abuse, spittle bubbling on his lips, his discoloured complexion a mass of grey blotches, he dragged himself up and down the concrete chamber denouncing them all as traitors. He said that the Army General Staff should be hanged "to the last craven coward," that he had been betrayed by a conspiracy of "treason, corruption, and lies," and that he was done with the lot of them; they could sink or swim without him.

When Jodl summoned up the nerve to speak the Führer turned on him with all the viciousness of a rabid dog. "If the German people are to be conquered in the struggle," he spat in Jodl's face, "then they are too weak to face the test of history and are fit only for destruction. We shall not surrender. We shall never capitulate, no never! We may be destroyed, but if we are we shall drag half the world with us—a world in flames. There will be no one left to triumph over Germany."

Bormann, I could see, was in a funk of indecision. He was wringing his hands and nervously avoiding the inflamed stare from those blue-grey demonic eyes, now filmed with a haze of exhaustion.

"We must go south," he kept whining. "Within hours all the escape routes will be cut off. We must go south to

Obersalzberg and set up new command headquarters. It is the only hope. We must go south."

Hitler stood stock-still (as still as it is possible to be when the entire left side of the body—face, arm, leg—is twitching uncontrollably) and fixed Bormann with a terrible madman's glare.

"I will never leave Berlin—*never!* I have taken up an immovable position. I cannot change it. I shall take over the defence of Berlin but I shall not fall into enemy hands alive or dead. I will shoot myself and have my body burnt. It is all over, finished. The Third Reich is no more. I shall stay in Berlin and wait to meet the end."

Jodl, Keitel and Krebs were plainly distressed at this. They looked at one another in the manner of three bewildered schoolboys who have just been informed by the headmaster that henceforth they will have to teach themselves. Jodl spread his hands piteously. "But what are we to do? After you have been directing and leading us for so long how can you suddenly send us away and expect us to lead ourselves? It is not possible."

"What are we to do without you?" asked Krebs, and Keitel looked on blankly, totally bemused and bewildered. They were three lost sheep.

The Führer was supporting himself on the corner of the table, his knuckles pressing whitely and his breathing shallow and quick like an animal with one leg caught fast in a steel trap. He said in a low voice, all the strength and resolve drained out of it:

"I have no orders to give you. If you require orders then you should seek them from the Reich Marshal."

Krebs blinked and stepped back at these astounding words. "There isn't a single German soldier who would fight under the Reich Marshal," he said.

"There is no question of fighting now," Hitler said, astounding them even more. "There is nothing left to fight with. If it's a question of negotiating, Goering can do that better than I."

This, plainly, was a bombshell, and the dank concrete room was filled with an unbearable claustrophobic silence. But even worse was to follow. While we were still taking in the enormity of these momentous utterances a courier arrived with a top secret message. Hitler read it and his eyes started to bulge out of his head. He choked and gasped for breath and I had to steady him to prevent his legs giving away completely. The paper fluttered out of his hand and Jodl picked it up and read it aloud.

Mein Führer!

In view of your decision to remain at your post in the fortress of Berlin, do you agree that I take over, at once, the total leadership of the Reich, with full freedom of action at home and abroad, as your deputy, in accordance with your decree of 29th June 1941? If no reply is received by ten o'clock tonight I shall take it for granted that you have lost your freedom of action, and shall consider the conditions of your decree as fulfilled, and shall act for the best interests of our country and our people. You know what I feel for you in this gravest hour of my life. Words fail me to express myself. May god protect you and speed you quickly here in spite of all.

Your loyal—
Hermann Goering.

I led the Führer to a chair and he sagged into it like a puppet whose strings have snapped. His eyes were glazed and rivulets of sweat, shining on his neck like slug's trails, had soaked into the collar of his shirt. I ordered one of the adjutants to fetch my bag and waved the others back to give him air, chill and stuffily damp as it was.

He raised his head and his slack wet mouth worked uselessly. I told him to remain calm and not to excite himself further, but he would insist, through pale tight lips, on attempting to speak.

"Hermann Goering has betrayed both me and the Fatherland," he croaked hoarsely. "Behind my back he has plotted to usurp the authority vested in me by God and the German people. His action is a mark of cowardice."

"Mein Führer—" I started to say.

"And against my orders he has sent me a disrespectful message, saying that I once named him as my successor, and that now, since I can no longer rule from Berlin, he is ready to rule from Berchtesgaden in my place."

"Do not upset yourself," I said soothingly, filling a syringe with 50 mg. of dextromoramide mixed with 4 mg. of dihydromorphinone hydrochloride, a preparation of my own concoction that is the only thing these days that seems to have any effect on him. I shot the full load into his arm and he didn't even wince. "Calm yourself," I said, wiping a trickle of blood from the puncture hole. "It isn't important enough to work yourself into a tizz."

He choked and the muscles in his face went rigid. His blood-shot eyes, I noted, were filled with moisture.

"An ultimatum!" he suddenly screeched at the top of his voice. "A crass ultimatum! Nothing now remains, nothing is spared, no loyalty is kept, no honour observed. There is no bitterness, no betrayal that has not been heaped upon me—and now this! It is the end. No injury has been left undone!"

"Yes, yes," I consoled him, patting him on the shoulder. "It really is a crying shame."

The ceremony took place at 2.40 in the morning on 29th April. It was a simple affair, held in the map room adjoining Hitler's study, officiated over by somebody in the uniform of the Volkssturm and attended by several people including Goebbels, Bormann, myself and two secretaries.

As she was about to go through from her bedroom Eva caught my arm and hissed under her breath, "I never thought it would go this far. You never mentioned marriage. I'm stuck with him for life now!"

"You make it sound like for ever," I smiled, squeezing her left buttock. "Life can be long or life can be short."

Eva frowned at me and I gave her a broad wink.

As she was signing the register the bride was about to write "Eva B—" She glanced at me from under her eyelashes and crossed out the B and wrote instead "Eva Hitler, née Braun."

Berlin, 1st May, 1945
I cannot believe it. It isn't true. The whole thing is as topsy-turvy as a fairy-tale.

Who should suddenly appear in the Führerbunker this morning but Nicolaus von Below, Wehrmachtattaché (Luftwaffe) on a mission of the most vital importance. He had piloted a Focke-Wulf 190 from Rechlin, dodging Russian fighters and surviving an intensive air barrage on the way, and managed to make Gatow, the last remaining Berlin airfield in Allied hands. At Gatow he had commandeered a light training aircraft and flown into the city at tree-top level, intending to land in the Wilhelmstrasse, within walking distance of the Chancellery. Hit by Russian anti-aircraft fire above the Grunewald, he had sustained a wound in the right shoulder but had succeeded in landing the aircraft and making his way to the Bunker through the ruins of the Reich Chancellery.

I was attending the Führer when he was admitted, giving him the first of his eight daily injections; Eva was there too, still in her night attire, and the three of us were taken aback by von Below's miraculous appearance, out of the blue as it were. His wounded arm had been hastily dressed and put in a sling and even so he made a commendable attempt at saluting with his left hand, snapping to attention and clicking his heels, which brought a spasm of pain to his face.

The cerebral stimulant I had just administered to the Führer was beginning to take effect, overcoming the chloral hydrate which allowed him to snatch a few hours' sleep, and he sat up on the bed, his dulled gaze seeking out the newcomer. I propped him up with pillows and wiped a smear of saliva from his chin.

"Mein Führer!" began von Below, staring fixedly ahead

at the concrete wall. "This is a great and glorious day for the Fatherland. I b-b-bring you tidings of great joy: the salvation of the Reich!"

"Yes, very well," I said, waving my hand. "Get on with it."

He was struggling to extricate an envelope from his inner pocket, making heavy weather of it due to his injured arm and shoulder.

I sighed ponderously. "Come along, we haven't got all day."

"This message—" von Below said, at last pulling it out "—this message has been entrusted to me b-b-by the—"

"Good God, man," I said peremptorily, "can't you even speak properly? What's the matter with you, are you a cretin?"

He shook his head. "N-N-No—"

"Then get on with it, get on with it! The Führer is waiting."

He handed the envelope to me and I opened it. Inside there was a single sheet of flimsy grey paper, unheaded, containing perhaps a dozen typewritten lines. I held it in front of the Führer's face and he stared at it uncomprehendingly for several moments.

"Oh dear," I said, glancing at Eva. "I think he's gone again."

"Give him another shot," she said. "A big one."

"I've just given him double the usual dose. He should be leaping around like a spring lamb."

Eva groaned. "Anything but that; he might start getting ideas."

I crumpled the sheet of paper into a ball and stuck it in my pocket. "You'd better give it to him direct," I told von Below. "He's forgotten his reading glasses."

"The Führer wears glasses?" he said, astounded.

"The message?" I suggested, very softly. "Could we possibly, do you suppose, hear the message?"

"Oh yes." Von Below clicked his heels. "Mein Führer! I have the proud honour to inform you that at long last, after many years of patient and dedicated research by German scientists, the Atomic B-B-Bomb is now at the service of the Reich. All difficulties have been overcome and the wonder weapon is at this moment capable of being delivered to any point on the globe and successfully d-d-detonated. I have been commanded by General Koller, Chief of Staff of the Luftwaffe, to inform you that the Bomb is on board an aircraft which is standing b-b-by awaiting your instructions. With mid-flight refuelling we have an unlimited range of operation. General Koller only wishes to know the t-t-target you have selected for the first atomic explosion in the history of the human race."

"Is that it?" I inquired. "Have you done?"

"My mission is c-c-completed," von Below said, saluting and clicking once more. "Heil Hitler! God save the Reich!"

"He does go on, doesn't he?" Eva said, filing her nails.

"Did you hear that, mein kleiner Misthaufen*?" I said, waving my hand in front of the Führer's face. "We have the Bomb. The B-O-M-B. We can drop it anywhere we like. Pick a city."

Hitler suddenly jerked upright and a gob of mucus fell on the bed. He was looking into the top corner of the room with absolute concentration, no doubt seeing glorious visions of the thousand-year future.

"Historical Necessity and Justice," he said in a high tremulous tone, so unlike his normal voice that I looked round to see who was speaking. Eva raised her eyes to heaven and carried on filing her nails.

"We shall win through to ultimate victory," the Führer continued, a semblance of colour returning to his cheeks. "German science and German might shall triumph in the end. *We are indestructible!*"

Von Below, it seemed, was fired by this outburst, for into his eyes came a gleam of fanatical zeal. "Picture it, mein Führer, the charred b-b-bodies and the creeping radiation sickness. C-C-Cancer of the blood cells for generation after

*My little dungheap.

generation. Babies deformed in the womb. A race of mu-mu-mutants with bent limbs and twisted brains. An entire land, an entire people, reduced to crawling subservience. The establishment of a truly Aryan m-m-master race!''

Hitler was nodding, spittle drooling from his lips (Apropos of this, I've often noticed that when he talks a dry whitish powdery substance forms at the corners of his mouth, as though his body was excreting poison of some sort. Most odd.)

Now the Führer was burbling to himself, von Below leaning forward and straining to catch the mumbled wisdom of the greatest military strategist of all time, the Messiah of the German people, Godhead of the Teutonic Soul.

''Ho-hum,'' Eva said, patting her curls into place in the mirror.

''Thank you for delivering the message,'' I said to von Below. ''Most courageous and loyal of you. The Führer, as you can see, is delighted. You will be suitably rewarded. Good day.''

Von Below tore his eyes away from the Führer and stared at me. His jaw went up and down. ''B-B-B-B-B-But—''

''Thank you so much,'' I sang out. ''There's the door. Nice of you to call.''

''B-B-But the B-B-Bomb,'' he stuttered, looking at me, then at Hitler, then at me again. ''General Koller is awaiting the Führer's instructions. We must d-d-decide on a target and issue an ultimatum at once. There is no t-t-time to lose.''

''And no time will be lost,'' I assured him. ''But as you can see, the Führer is rather overcome at the moment. When he has rested and his mind is cleared he will be much more able to make a sensible decision. We mustn't rush these things.''

''But General K-K-Koller is wai—''

''Are you questioning the medical advice of the Führer's personal physician?'' I asked, thunderstruck. ''Are you prepared to gamble with the Führer's life? Is this treason I hear? Are you insane? Do you want to be put in front of a firing-squad?''

"No, no." Von Below retreated a step or two, his eyes blinking in alarm. "I didn't realize." He saluted and clicked his heels. "Forgive me, mein Führer. My abject apologies. I shall wait outside for your d-d-decision." He turned to go.

I said, "You will leave the Führerbunker at once and return to Rechlin. Frau Junge will see to it that you have a packed lunch to take with you."

Von Below gaped at me. "F-F-F-Fly back? To Rechlin? But how?"

"The same way you came. Over the Russian lines."

"I will be shot down. There is a solid wall of anti-aircraft fire surrounding the city."

"You got here," I pointed out, not unreasonably I thought.

"But I had a fighter escort as far as Gatow. They diverted the b-b-barrage but even so I was hit. It will be madness to return. Suicide."

"Nevertheless you must leave immediately," I informed him. "It is the Führer's wish that you report back on the success of your mission to General Koller. Tell him that everything is in hand."

"I heard the Führer say nothing to that effect."

"He whispered it. You were busy saluting at the time and didn't hear him. Good-bye."

"B-B-B-B-B—"

"Good," I said, "Bye."

When he had gone I patted Hitler on the head and said, "There we are, kränklicher Knose*, all taken care of; nothing to worry about."

"New York," he croaked, staring into the corner of the room, his breath coming faster. "We will devastate New York as a warning." He turned his gaze slowly towards me. "Summon Sturmbannführer Guensche. I wish to dictate a message, top priority."

"He is already here."

"Good, all is well," Hitler murmured. "Guensche!"

"Yes, mein Führer."

*Sickly man-child.

"Send this message, top priority, to General Koller."

"Yes, mein Führer."

"Instruct him to detonate the Bomb over New York *without any warning whatsoever to the military or civilian authorities*. When this has been carried out I shall require immediate confirmation so that I can issue an ultimatum. Is that perfectly clear?"

"Yes, mein Führer."

Hitler's grey haggard blotchy features relaxed into something that might have been a smile. "When they realize that we possess the ultimate weapon there will be no alternative left open to them but total and abject surrender. It is Historical Necessity and Justice." He jerked his head, almost in the old manner. "Guensche: send the message to General Koller without delay."

"Very good, mein Führer," I said, clicking my heels.

"Oh Jesus," Eva said, "he's completely over the top. Lock him up and throw away the key."

I opened my bag and took out a 500 mg. bottle of trichlorethylene and a gauze pad. I soaked the pad in the solution, holding it well away from my face, and returned the bottle to the bag.

Eva frowned at me through the dressing-table mirror. "What are you doing?"

"Just something to relax him. His nerves are on edge."

"What an awful smell," she said, wrinkling her nose.

"It is rather strong," I said, "but extremely effective."

I pushed him back against pillows and held the gauze pad to his face. His bloodshot eyes, the broken blood-vessels like cracks, stared straight at me for what seemed a long time, without fear or panic, and then crossed. The lids drooped and closed. He didn't struggle or twitch a muscle. I kept the pad there a while longer and put it away in my bag.

"Is he out?" asked Eva.

"Like a baby."

"Thank God for that." She was humming to herself and examining the lines round her eyes. "He bores the arse off me, Theo."

"He bores the arse off most people," I said, taking the Luger automatic pistol out of the bag and checking the clip. Eva was preoccupied with her face and didn't pay any attention as I put the barrel of the pistol into his mouth and with my other hand arranged the pillows over the top in a kind of soft white mound, like a snow castle, and pulled the trigger. There was a low dull thud, not terribly loud, and a few feathers flew into the air and floated about.

Eva turned and looked at me. She looked at the door. She said, "Did. . . ?"

I smiled and shook my head. "Nobody heard."

"Is he dead?"

"Of course he's fucking dead," I said, withdrawing my arm from the mound of pillows and dropping the pistol on the bed. The barrel was smeared with bits of red and grey stuff. "What do you think I used, a pea-shooter? The back of his head's gone."

"Oh Theo," she said, running to me. "Theo."

"It's all right," I calmed her, stroking her shoulders, "they'll think it's suicide. I'll make it look that way. No need to worry or get upset."

"I'm not upset. I'm not."

I patted her and smiled reassuringly. "Just take this." I reached down into the bag and took out a vial containing a dozen bluish-colored capsules. Eva at once looked frightened. "Don't be afraid, there's no need."

"What are they? What are they for?" Her breathing was light and fluttery. She was staring at the vial.

I led her across to the small sofa and we sat down. "Now listen carefully. These capsules are a mild extraction of cocaine. When you take them you will lose consciousness for, oh, a couple of hours or so. While you are unconscious I will tell Guensche, Kempka and the others that you and the Führer have taken your own lives. However—" I held up my finger "—I will make an attempt to revive you by using Ultraseptyl and of course I will succeed. In that way they can't blame you for having survived when the Führer has perished. It will not be your fault that the drug didn't act swiftly enough."

"Oh Theo, do I have to?"

"Of course you have to. How else can we explain the situation to them? And just think, mein kleines Entchen*, think of it— from tomorrow we shall always be together, you and I. Always and for ever!"

Eva pressed herself to me and I could feel her body trembling. She said, "Love me, Theo. I need your strength."

"There will be plenty of time for that later. We shall have all eternity together."

"You must love me now, then I'll know that you truly love me. Please, Theo!"

So I had to curb my impatience and waste precious time making love to her on the sofa. The fabric made my knees sore. I knew that any minute Kempka or Linge or one of the others might decide to inquire if the Führer was in need of anything; they would not enter unless bidden but even so their suspicions might be aroused. Anyway, I thought, what the hell. What would a few minutes more matter to destiny?

We pumped away and sweated at it for a while and turning my head and brushing her damp hair out of my eyes I could see the mound of pillows speckled with red, the ones near the bottom soaking it up like dark heavy wine. The Führer's legs stuck out at ridiculous angles, the feet splayed, and I recalled that he always was flat-footed.

Eva clung to me and whimpered as I released myself inside her. She laid her head on my chest and told me she loved me.

"I love you too," I said, looking at my watch.

"How did you get this?" she asked. "Is it a birthmark?" She touched the faint scar below my left shoulder, the pale indented tissue like that of a brand. "You've never told me what it is or how you got it."

"A memento of long ago. Nothing important. I'll tell you all about it some other time."

*My little duckling.

"Oh I do love you, Theo."

"So you keep saying." I pushed her away and sat up. "Now you must take the capsules, there isn't much time."

"How many must I take?"

"All of them," I said, emptying the dozen capsules into the palm of my hand. She took them, one by one, washing them down with water, and I laid her on the sofa, arranging her limbs neatly. Three tablets wouldn't have done her much harm, five would have knocked her out, but all twelve would produce a toxic effect of palpitations, vomiting, convulsions, rapid pulse rate, circulatory collapse, crawling of the flesh, and eventually death. The whole process took about ten minutes.

While I waited for the end I took out my special brand, manufactured only for me, and at the same time remembered the crumpled piece of paper in my pocket: setting fire to it I inhaled deeply on the Nexus-T and watched the paper burn itself to flimsy grey ash.

10

Minus Time

Karla Ritblat was satisfied with the patient's progress and on the seventeenth day he was transferred from Psycho-Med to one of the seclusion rooms into which sunlight could be introduced at any time of the day. Sometimes it was too much of a good thing and the omni-directional reflectors were turned away so that the room was bathed in cool pleasant shade.

He was less pale now, though his eyes still shone with a curious translucence; it would be at least a week before his metabolic rate returned to a level which could be regarded as normal.

On his first day out of intensive care Karla Ritblat told him that he would be allowed visitors but warned that if the Neuron Processor registered any abnormal activity, no matter how slight, she would have no hesitation in putting him straight back into hyper-suspension.

"Another fortnight in the jelly bag," Queghan said, winking at her. "You'd like that."

"It's for your benefit, not mine," Karla Ritblat responded primly. "You don't suppose I do it for my own amusement."

"You're all heart," Queghan said, watching her as she went to the door. Karla Ritblat set her lips so as not to smile. She went out of the room without looking at him, saying over her shoulder:

"And no smoking. Those dreadful tube things upset the EEG and they're positively bad for you."

"No ma'am. Yes ma'am."

During the morning Karve came down from Level 40 and brought with him Pouline deGrenier and Léon Steele. The Director glided into the room and brought his chair to the foot of the bed, saying with a small cryptic smile, "Returned to the land of the living, I see."

"How long have you been ill?" Pouline said. She couldn't understand why he was in bed. "Did you know?" she said to Léon.

Léon shook his head, and his eyes were so large and appealing, fully upon her, that Pouline had to turn away. She found it embarrassing to look at him: his entire manner implied a special intimacy that she herself didn't feel. It was even rather insulting, for she had never given him cause to expect or hope for anything on a deeper, more personal level.

"Chris suffers from a complaint that doctors used to call epilepsy," Karve said. "It can be controlled—sometimes—though it's rather an erratic affair. In its controlled state we call it mythic projection."

"You've been into mythic projection?" Léon Steele said, moving nearer to the bed. He studied Queghan closely.

"So they tell me."

"Don't you know yourself?"

"It's all rather vague, a bit dreamlike. Some details are clear while others are shadowy and unreal." He looked at Pouline. "Professor deGrenier knows what I mean."

"Do I?" she said, startled.

"Sometimes it's difficult to separate what actually happened from what might have happened. You know the feeling."

"Yes, I suppose so," Pouline said uncertainly. She was frowning. "How long have you been here—in Psycho-Med, I mean?"

"Couple of weeks."

"Weeks?"

"Doesn't time fly?" Queghan said. His eyes, oddly illuminated from within, were fixed on hers with a peculiar intensity; so intense that for a moment the room swam inside her head and the slats of sunlight seemed to slide down the wall.

Léon broke in to say, smiling brightly, "Just as well we didn't need your help." He held up a thick folder encased in a vinyl wrapper. "We sorted out the problem with RECONPAN."

"I'm glad to hear that," Queghan said, careful not to catch the Director's eye. For the moment they avoided looking at each other.

Léon went on eagerly, "It wasn't the hardware to blame at all, it was the program. I spotted it at once when I checked the Subject Profile. Some of the research input was wrong—the file on Dr. Morell. You remember him?"

"Vividly," Queghan said.

Léon sat down on the side of the bed. "What I did was this: I asked the facility to list the personnel in the Führerbunker from 22nd April to 1st May, 1945—"

"And it missed someone out."

"No, no," Léon said. "It included someone who shouldn't have been there: Theodor Morell."

"Morell wasn't in the Bunker?" Queghan said.

"According to Archives he left the Bunker in the middle of April, the seventeeth I think it was." He held the folder aloft, gleeful as a schoolboy. "And this confirms it!"

"Oh yes?" Queghan said. "What is it?"

"You recall how we couldn't get the cyberthetic system to give us any biographical information on Morell? It occurred to me that what had actually happened was that somehow or other the system had become confused with real-life historical Morells and fictional Morells. Somehow a circuit had cross-connected itself and as a result we'd fed a lot of spurious and misleading data into the RECONPAN facility. Little wonder the brain was confused."

"Little wonder," Queghan agreed.

"So what did you do?" asked Karve.

"Simple," Léon said, his face alight. "I asked the cyberthetic system to give me a *fictional* account by or about somebody called Morell. And it came up with this, no problem at all, pages and pages of it."

"Of what?" said Queghan and Karve together.

"The Diaries of Dr. Morell." Léon took the folder from the vinyl wallet and opened it. "It's all here, the missing information. I fed it into the facility and it all fits perfectly. Isn't that right, Pouline?"

Pouline deGrenier was looking at Queghan as though expecting the answer to a riddle to appear suddenly on his face.

"May I see?" Queghan took the folder and glanced at the first page. He almost smiled.

"What does it say?" Karve asked.

Queghan read:

" 'Berlin, July 1938. The trees looked lovely this morning as I walked along the Wilhelmstrasse on my way to the Chancellery. The city gardeners perform an excellent service in keeping the place neat and trim and shipshape. It was a pleasure to be abroad on such a fine morning.

" 'A tedious incident which took the edge off my good humour and benign disposition: one of the guards, presumably new on the duty roster, stood in my way and asked to see my papers. He obviously didn't know who I was and remained obdurate when I informed him that I was a member of the Sanctum.' "

"What do you think?" said Karve. "Is it authentic?"

"Absolutely." Queghan glanced through several pages and said to Léon, "Is there any mention of the atomic bomb?"

"The Germans never got anywhere near testing it. They knew how to produce a radioactive material called *U235* but they hadn't the technology to make it in sufficient quantity for a bomb. It wasn't till thirty years later that the technique was developed on a commercial scale."

"I'm glad that you're convinced," Pouline said to Queghan.

Queghan handed the folder to Léon. "History is full of surprises. The reality is never how you imagine it to be."

"Do you mean the probability of history?" Pouline said.

There was a ghost of a smile on her face. "Isn't it true to say that your being in Psycho-Med for the past two weeks is as much a probability as a fact? You might have been here and you might have been somewhere else. The number of places you *might* have been is infinite."

"I don't follow that," Léon said, frowning. He absently pulled at a finger-joint. "Either he was here or he wasn't here. A thing happens or it doesn't happen." But even as he was saying this he thought of the night he had spent with Pouline. Had it really taken place or was it just his imagination? Sometimes fantasy was more vivid than reality. He wasn't at all sure any longer.

Karve turned his chair towards the door. "Do you have the original RECONPAN report on file—a complete record of everything the facility came up with?"

"We never destroy anything," Léon said. "Would you like to see it?"

"I'm curious as to how far the mythical Führer got with his plans to drop an atomic bomb on New York." The Director smiled. "Should make a good story by the sound of it."

Queghan said, "He was probably foiled in the end by the hero."

Karla Ritblat came into the room and paused in mid-stride. She said warningly, "Remember what I told you. If the Processor registers the slightest shift you're back in Psycho-Med."

"Yes ma'am." Queghan lay back against the pillows. He did look tired and washed out, Pouline deGrenier thought. His hands were like alabaster.

"Karla can't wait to try her new wonder remedy on me. Dr. Koester's Antigas Pills. Guaranteed to cure everything under the sun."

"What an odd coincidence," Léon said. "If you read the Diaries you'll find that—"

"We shouldn't bother the mythographer with our tedious research," Pouline said to her assistant.

"I'm sorry." Léon stood up and smoothed the covers. "I hope you get better very soon."

They were about to leave, chivvied along by Karla Ritblat's officious manner and bleak stare, when a woman came tentatively into the room and looked at them wonderingly. She had bright red lips, dark eyes ringed with blue shadows, and blond hair swept up on top of her head and held in place by a silver comb inlaid with onyx.

She said hesitantly, "Mr. Spade?"

Everyone looked at her blankly.

"The receptionist was out so I came straight in."

"I don't think—" Karla Ritblat began.

"I was told I might find Mr. Spade here."

"Yes," Queghan said. "That would be me. Sit down, sweetheart."

Pouline deGrenier couldn't understand why he was lisping.

"What's the problem, blue eyes?" Queghan said.

"Well, Mr. Spade—"

"Who is this person?" Karla Ritblat asked.

"Be quiet," Karve said.

"It's this man, he keeps following me." The woman took out a dainty lace-trimmed handkerchief and sniffed into it. There was a stifled sob in her voice which spilled out into: "I think he wants to kill me."

"Okay, okay," Queghan said. "No need to get upset. It don't surprise me that some guy is following you. You're a swell-looking chick."

"Thank you, Mr. Spade."

"Call me Sam."

"I was told that you might be able to help me."

"I'm your man," Queghan said, stroking his lower lip and smiling at her lopsidedly. "I can help you all right." He crooked his forefinger under her chin and lifted her head. "Hey," he said, "enough of that. Here's looking at you, kid."

Somewhere in the black wastes of space there is a species of sub-atomic particles which possesses cosmic intelligence. Collectively, in their billions, they have the ability to move through a region of minus time, to infiltrate entire galaxies, to affect energy and matter and the curvature of space itself.

Their intelligence is not of the human order: it is timeless and infinite, aware of the space surrounding it only in the way that neurons in the human brain are conscious of the permeable fluid membrane which contains them.

These particles are the Hadrons. Their life-cycle is the history of the universe, from the beginning to the end of time. Their consciousness is beyond good and evil, above moral sway. They are the purest form of intelligence extant in the whole of Creation.

At some point in the distant past—and in the mythical future—the Hadrons have and will come into contact with human life-forms. Their influence is negligible and catastrophic.

The Hadrons can distort spacetime, upset the earthbound order of cause and effect, alter historical sequence, and enter into human consciousness. They manifest themselves in ways beyond the compass of man-made technology and comprehension—but not, occasionally, of human intuition.

The Hadrons are alive in the universe, somewhere in spacetime. Beware the next coincidence.

Appendix

Causality

In the everyday world we are so used to the phenomenon known as causality (Cause and Effect) that it takes a real effort of the imagination to visualize how the universe could function sensibly without it. For example we would think it ludicrous for someone to sustain an injury *and then* to have the accident which caused it. Or for a cup to shatter *before* it fell to the floor. Yet in the sub-atomic world of quantum mechanics similar strange happenings do occur—leading to even stranger theories as to the nature of time (linked indissolubly with causality), the ultimate reality of energy and matter, and the "laws" of probability.

The theoretical work which first questioned our unthinking acceptance of causality was carried out in the 1920s by physicists whose inspiration had come—of course—from Einstein. The line of thought passed through Bohr, de Broglie, Bose, Dirac, Schrödinger, and came to fulfilment in a twenty-three-year-old German physicist, Werner Heisenberg. He proposed that the quantum world—the world inside the atom—is by its very nature unobservable. If we wish to know, say, the position and momentum of a single particle we must bombard it with photons (particles of light) in order to observe it. But by doing so we are changing the nature of that which is being observed. Heisenberg concluded that we cannot *at the same time* know precisely where the particle is and how fast it is moving. One or the other—not both together.

This in itself is not world-shattering. But extend the idea

and what do we find? That if we lack information on where a particle is and how it is moving we also lack the means of predicting where it will be later on. The future of that single particle is thus not definite but *probabilistic*, and therefore causality is in doubt. This has become known as the Principle of Indeterminacy and is the cornerstone of much of the thought in theoretical physics and metaphysics in the mid-Twentieth.

When the theory was put forward Einstein instinctively rebelled against it. He couldn't believe—he refused to believe—that God could create a universe of probability in which the fate of each individual particle was left to chance; he summed up his belief in the famous phrase "Gott würfelt nicht": "God does not play dice."

Another concept which has had a profound effect on our everyday notion of causality came as a direct consequence of Einstein's Theory of Relativity. The mathematics are difficult to understand and so we have to take on trust the physicist's conclusion, which is indeed world-shattering. Briefly stated, it is that there is no universal time providing a universal simultaneity. In other words time is not a universal constant but, by its very nature, is *relative to the position and velocity of the observer*. What this means is that two observers, A and B, moving at different speeds, would find that events which are simultaneous for A are not simultaneous for B, and vice verse.

Thus we might find that while A strenuously maintained that event *x* happened before event *y*, observer B, with equal fervour, would say that event *y* came before event *x*. Which one is right? The answer is that both of them are—because the simultaneity of separated events moving at different speeds is relative. There is no universal constant by which we can measure who is right and who is wrong.

And once we go along with the theory we find some extremely bizarre happenings which outrage our everyday common sense. Just as time is relative to the individual observer, so are length, distance, speed, acceleration, force, and energy. We can only measure any of these accurately as they pertain to our own frame of reference. To another observer they will appear quite different—and again both sets of measurements are equally valid. This leads to such baffling contradictions as A observing the time-scale of B and finding it slower than his own (which is what would happen if they were moving at significantly different speeds); yet when B observes the time-scale of A he too finds it slower than his own. And both are correct within their individual parameters of observation.

As someone once said, "Everything is either constantly relative or relatively constant: and it don't matter much which."